T0128866

Agatha and Frank Living the Dream

Living the Dream

JOLYNN ROSE

Trafford rev.   11/07/2016

 www.trafford.com

North America & international
toll-free: 1 888 232 4444 (USA & Canada)
fax: 812 355 4082

PROLOGUE

Frank and Agatha (Aggie) have been married for over thirty-eight years. They have three children and the family is starting to grow. Their oldest is Frank Jr.; he has been married to Wanda for two years. Their daughters Twila and Maria have been dating the same men for a few years.

It was time for Frank and Aggie to start the next chapter of their lives. Frank Sr. and Aggie loved to sail and their dream was to sail around the Atlantic Ocean when they retired. Island hopping is what they called it. Aggie retired from being a history teacher a few years ago, and Frank finally retired from the Army.

The next month they were on their sailboat heading out into the great blue water. The first few months were wonderful; there were a few problems with their boat before they took off. But they had the boat for about five years, so they knew her very well. They named their boat "Big Dream,"

Frank had to name every vehicle and boat they owned. All boats have to have a name anyway, Right. Why not vehicles too? He named the Jeep, "Toad."

Frank wasn't too happy about all the problems, but Aggie being a positive person, just kept telling him, "Better now, than out on the ocean." Frank had to agree with her again, but would always say, "I can still complain about it!" They would both tease each other and then agree and move on.

The reason I pointed this out is because they ended up getting shipwrecked on an island for five and a half years. They rescued themselves, by finding a boat and fixing it up. They had a lot of help from the Roslanders; the natives of the island. Let's just say, Merbeings do exist! That is another story. This book is about the adventures Frank and Aggie had traveling across the United States.

After Frank and Aggie had been back for an awhile, the grandkids talked them into going on a road trip with the whole family. By now the family had grown, Frank Jr. and Wanda had two boys, Daniel and Douglas. Twila married Dennis and had two girls; Tina, Sharlene, and Maria married James and had two girls also, Treva and Enola. They all traveled from Houston, TX to Eureka, CA and back to Houston. Everyone had a great time and a lot of fun. This story is about **Agatha and Frank, and their Road Trip Adventure**. They are going to live their Dream!

After returning from their road trip with their family, they all settled into everyday life. They did some sailing around the bay and over to Florida and Mexico. They also enjoyed hanging out with their family and friends. But the road was calling them back for another road trip adventure. They had both been in the Army. Aggies spend seven years in the Army, and then she left to become a History teacher.

Frank continued his career in the Army. So after three years they started getting a little antsy, which was how long they normally stayed at one post. Needless to say, **Frank and Agatha, Is on the Road Again!**

CHAPTER 1

July 17

Frank and Agatha got in late last night, so Agatha (Aggie) slept in late this morning, and she did sleep like a rock. When she woke up Frank was already out of bed. He hadn't said anything the night before about going anywhere in the morning. So it was a surprise that Frank wasn't anywhere to be found, so she went looking for him. Aggie walked over to Frankie's Jr. house's to see if Frank Sr. was over there but he wasn't. Frankie had a big grin on his face which always meant something was up. She tried to get it out of him, but he wasn't having anything to do with it. He just told her, "Dad will tell you when he gets back!" She knew something was up, she went looking for Wanda; she figured she could get it out of her. But Wanda wouldn't have anything to do with it either. When Aggie (Grandma) looked at the boys, they took off running and plugged their ears. As if they couldn't hear her.

Frankie told her to be patient and she'll see soon enough what Dad was up to. Aggie went back to their house and waited for Frank to come home. As she waited her mind was going a mile a minute trying to figure out what Frank was up to. But she had no clue what he might be up to.

Aggie heard Frank's truck pull up to the house, she was determined not to get up and greet him. When Frank finally opened the door to the house, two little dogs came running through the door. The first thing they did was jump on her lap and wiggled their little butts, like they were her best friends. She couldn't believe it, that Frank had gone and got the dogs that they had looked at earlier during the week. He just stood there with a big smile on his face, and said, "Meet your new kids! This delivery is easier than the last three you had." Aggie looked at Frank and he said, "Well, you said you wanted a dog, now we each have one! Now all we need to do is get a RV, so we can travel around this country of ours!"

The dogs were both mutts. One was black and white, and one was brown and white. The people at the pet store said, "They were a terrier mix, and there's a little bit of something else in them, they didn't know what. It was a mother and daughter; their names are Sheba and Susie." Susi weighed about 12 pounds and Sheba weighed about 8 pounds, she was smaller than Susi. They are just so full of love, and they wanted to share it with them.

Aggie was so delighted, she couldn't stop smiling. She turned to their new pets, Sheba and Susie, and said "Well what do you think? Do you think you will like traveling around in a RV?" They started wagging their tails and jumping around. She looked at Frank and told him she guessed that meant yes! Frank agreed, and replied, "Let's go tell Frankie Jr. and his family. Aggie said, "I'm sure they will like this idea better than us going out on another boat trip. Aggie laughed; as she told the dogs to come on, let's go meet the family.

The dogs ran to the door and started barking. Aggie figured they were not moving fast enough for them. She opened the door, and off they went. Frank took off after them, yelling "Come here, Stop and calling their names. They finally stopped and looked at Frank. They both looked at him, with a look of "What?" Frank stopped too, and called to them, "Come here Sheba and Susie." They both looked at each other and walked back to Frank and sat down. Frank and Aggie couldn't help but laugh and picked them up. They didn't what to take a chance of them taking off again. They headed over to Frankie and Wanda's house, to show off their new traveling partners.

Frankie and Wanda lived next door, in fact Frank and Aggie lived in their guest house behind the main house. So they headed off to Frankie's, but they didn't even get to Frankie's house before their grandsons were already picking up the dogs. Aggie looked at Frank and said, "I think they were waiting for us. She kind of figured they had already known about the dogs. Their Grandpa had told them what he was up to earlier that week. So it wasn't a surprise for them.

They told Frankie and Wanda about their plans to get a travel trailer and start traveling around the country. The first thing Wanda said was, "Good, it is better than going out on another ocean trip. Frank smiled at Aggie and said, "I told you so! They knew Wanda would say something about the ocean travels. Aggie just smiled and agreed with Frank.

Frankie wanted to know when we would be going shopping for the RV. He said, "When you do go looking, let me know, I want to go!" Aggie spoke up and said how about tomorrow. They all agreed that would work. Frankie Jr. said, "I can't wait to hear what my sisters say. You know they're going to want to go with you on the trip." Aggie just replied, "Yeah, but they can't. Maybe they can join us once in awhile."

They called Twila and Maria and told them about their plans. Next thing they knew they were all having dinner at Twila's house (their daughter) talking about where they plan on going next. Aggie thought, "Here we go again!"

July 22

Frank had done the research about each of the types and cost, beforehand as usual. They had brochures everywhere, on every type of rig there were. Well they did it! Frank and Aggie purchased a Class A, RV. A Class A, recreational vehicle (RV), looks like a really nice bus. They learned more about RV's than they ever wanted to know.

Their RV is thirty feet long; it has one pull out, the couch and the kitchen pulled out two feet, which gave them a lot more room. It even has a bedroom, big TV up front, and it will sleep six. The colors inside are blue and green, with a leaf design.

They had borrowed a class A, RV from a friend on their first adventure traveling the Northwest with their family, last year. So they had a good idea about what will be required this time around. They would have to tow a car this time. But Aggie had it in the back of her mind, that maybe she would drive the car, once and awhile. This way she would have time to herself, and listen to the music she likes. But on the long drives it would be nice to tow the car.

They did discover that there are a lot of campgrounds by the docks. Aggie guessed they were not the only old people that liked to travel on land and water both. Of course, they had to buy all kinds of new things to go with the RV. Mostly kitchen things and lots of outdoors things. The list is too long to put in here. After going on their thirty day trip with the kids, they had a really good idea about what they needed. But now with the dogs they had to add a few more items, dog leashes, food, bed and other items. Aggie could tell that Frank was going to spoil the girls.

They purchased a decal of the United States for the rig. It will go on the outside of the rig. As they travel to each state, they stick the decal for that state on. The kit has a decal for each state, even Hawaii. They we're sure how they're were going to get the RV over there. But you never know with Frank and Agatha. They discussed about if they should fill in the states they had gone though with the kids. They finally agreed to fill them in, mostly because they had no plans of going that direction for a little while.

They invited the grandkids over for a camp out; they had parked the RV by their house. They had a great time with them! They talked about their trip they went on last year, each had their favorite part. So much had happened on their adventure, and they could have gone on all night. But they needed to get up early so they could go fishing in the morning. Sharlene pointed out, that they will need fresh fish and crab for their trip, everyone agreed. It's been a while since they had been out on the boat. Frank Sr. told Aggie, it will be nice to go out with the kids fishing before we headed out on the road. Aggie just smiled and agreed. Frank gave her a hug and a kiss on her forehead.

They plan on taking the dogs with them; it'll be the first time the dogs will be on a boat. They had no idea how the dogs would react to being on a boat. Tina and Sharlene said, "They will keep an eye on them and if they get sick they will even clean it up." Aggie agreed that would work, as long as she didn't have to clean up after the dogs!

Frank had purchased a telescope earlier that week so the kids could look for UFO's, he joked. The kids were taking turns using it. Tina said she saw a UFO by the moon. Of course, all the kids had to see it. Aggie never did! They finally sent the grandkids to bed, they all slept in tents.

Enola and Treva, the granddaughters, had gone to a Rock and Mineral show with their parents earlier that day. They had brought the stone they had gotten from the show with them. Enola showed Aggie the stands she had purchased for her stones to be displayed on. Enola had gotten the stands to hold her wonderful stones, which she has been collecting. Both of the girls were taking after their grandma. Aggie has been collecting stones for many years; she has her own little museum in her house. The grandkids would come over and the first thing they would do was to ask, "Did you get any new stones, Grandma?" Aggie normally, had found something new to add to her collection. Aggie loved that her grandkids enjoyed collecting rocks too!

Daniel and Douglas stayed up late watching the sky for a little while longer, and then they headed off to bed. Being the oldest grandkids, they felt they didn't have to go to bed when the little ones did. Which of course is the way it should be, Right?

It was time for Frank and Aggie to hit the sack. Earlier the grandkids asked them to sleep in their tents with them, but Grandpa told them "They were getting way too old to be sleeping on the ground, but the dogs would like to sleep with you." Besides they needed to test out their new bed in their RV, to make sure it was comfortable.

The next morning everyone was up bright and early and ready to spend the day on the ocean, fishing and playing in the bay. It ended up being a great day; they caught enough fish and crab for dinner that night and some left over for

Frank and Aggie to take on their trip. Their granddaughter Sharlene made sure they had enough for their trip.

Frank and Aggies's plan was to go on a test run, later this week. They are going to travel around Texas for the first month. That way they can still use their sailboat too. Twila and Dennis said they would sail it to wherever they wanted it and then just take it home, afterwards. Their other kids said they would too, if they wanted them too. All their kids loved to sail.

It's going to be an interesting change for them. Aggie felt the hard part will be missing their kids and grandkids. But when the grandkids are out of school, hopefully they will join them, for a visit. With both of Frank and Aggie in their early 60's, they figured they have a good ten years to travel where ever they wanted too. They both wanted to do some rock hounding and work in fossil digging around the states. Aggie used to go on fossil digs with her parents, it was one of the best memories she has of her childhood. She hopes that someday, she can take her grandkids on one.

Aggie is still keeping journals, and was ready to start a new journal about the next adventures they will have together.

Chapter 2

Leaning to travel with pets!

It has taken them a little while to get back on the road; they spent the summer in Texas and out on their boat. Traveling with dogs is a lot different than not having dogs. When they went with their kids on their road trip last year, they didn't have any pets. They laughed at how much work people would have to do because they had pets. Well now they have two new dogs, Sheba and Susie, they are both young, about two years old and have not been trained. Or should I say Frank and Aggie haven't been trained yet. The dogs pretty much tell them when to go to bed and when to get up. They let them know when it's time to go for a walk or play with them. It is just like having kids! They loved it!

One of their earlier trips was going out to a friend's house, to see how the dogs would behave. Their friend's had a little farm and a place for them to set up their RV.

The first time they set up their RV with the dogs, it was crazy. The dogs wanted to run off and play. Of course, they had to keep calling the dogs back, and then they would put the dogs in the RV, but they would bark until they couldn't stand it anymore. They finally gave up and took the girls (the dogs) for a walk; they figured the rig will still be there when they get back. They had a great time checking out everything. One thing for sure, Aggie knew they would get their exercise while they traveled with the dogs.

They discovered early on that the first thing they needed to do in the morning is take the dogs for a walk. The dogs were really good about leaving them alone while they slept but once they moved or spoke or made any sounds, as far as the girls were concerned it was time to get up. It only took them once to learn there was no time to set up the coffee pot, because the dogs wouldn't wait for them to set up the coffee pot. They would start barking and jumping around, until they headed towards the door. Now Aggie would set up the coffee pot the night before, and just plug it in, before they went on their walk. By the time they got back the coffee was ready.

After a few days at their friends place they discovered that they needed to put a little fence up, around the front of the motor home. Because the dogs would run off as soon as the door opened. They would have to yell for them to come back. They knew this wouldn't be an acceptable thing to happen at a RV campground. The fence worked great for the dogs and they now have an understanding. The dogs can go out the door, but have to wait for Aggie to put their leashes on them. Then they can take them for their walk in the campground. I'm not really sure who was walking who!!

While we were at our friends place we received a call from Frank Jr., he told Frank and Aggie, that Grandpa had a heart attack and may need to have heart surgery. Frank Sr. called his Mom, his brother Styles answered the phone, and Styles told him that their Mom was at the hospital, with their Dad. He told Frank that their Dad may need to go in for double by-pass surgery. They didn't know if he will make it through the surgery. Frank told him they were on their way. It will only take them a day and half to get there. Styles told them, that they needed to get there as soon as they could. They are planning to do the surgery in a couple days so that it would be okay. They wanted to make sure that he was strong enough to survive it. Frank and Aggie loaded everything up and headed to Eureka, CA.

Frank started to get into the driver's seat and Aggie stopped him. Aggie told Frank to let her drive until he calmed down, he agreed, needless to say he was pretty upset. About two hours later he said, he wanted to drive, he needed to take his mine off his Dad. They only stopped once because of the heavy fog, the only other time they stopped was for gas. Frank talked about his Dad as he drove; he knew he was up there in age, 83. But he still couldn't believe he was in the hospital, with a heart attack. His dad had started exercising and watching his diet the last few years.

The mountains still had snow on them and it was foggy in some spots. It was so foggy in one area they couldn't see any more than five feet in front of them. They had no clue where they were at; except they were in California. The weird thing was people were passing them. After a while they saw red and blue lights in front of them. Aggie told Frank there must be an accident up ahead of them. Frank replied, "Yea, it was probably one of those knuckle heads that passed us." As they got closer they could see a police car going back and forth across the lanes. He was slowing everyone down.

What a smart idea, they won't be any accidents in his county tonight. They decided to pull over for the night. It just wasn't worth the chance of getting in a car accident. But it was easier said than done, you couldn't see any exits until you were right on them. But they did manage to finally get off the road. They grabbed the dogs and took them for a quick walk, before going to bed. It was so cold out; you could see your breath. It was hard to believe that it was California.

Frank was still trying to keep it together. Frank and his dad are really close, and they got even closer at their last visit with him. It was great to see them talking to each other without fighting. There were a few years when they had their problems; they didn't even talk to each other except when Mom and Aggie forced them to talk to each other. Franks Mom always said, "It was just growing pains." Aggie guessed fathers and sons go through a time where the father feels like he isn't needed anymore. The son feels like the father still treats him like a little kid. Both are too hardheaded to admit to the other how they feel. Mothers and daughters do the same thing. Aggie knew with her girls that sometimes it was trying. She figured its nature's way of pushing the kids out of the nest and into their own world.

Anyway, they made the trip in pretty good time. They arrived in Eureka in a day and half, just like Frank said. All they could do once they arrived was to wait and pray for him! Frank's dad went into surgery and it took about eight hours before they could see him in recovery. The doctor said, "The surgery went well, now it will be up to him if he survives or not. As it turned out, he only had to stay in the hospital for a week. They told us that there wasn't anything else they could do for him at the hospital so they could take him home in a week. Frank's Dad told his wife that if he was going to go he wanted to spend his last days with her in their home!

After Frank and Aggie returned from the hospital, they set up the RV. Frank was by his father's side every moment he could be. His brother Style's was by his father side too. They took turns being with their father, talking to him and wiping his forehead. Aggie tried to help Frank's Mom as much as she could, she was so lost.

They released Dennis; Frank's Dad from the hospital and had settled him into his bedroom. As Lola and Aggie was making more coffee, Frank's Mom started telling Aggie what had happened at their house earlier. Lola told her, "He was just fine; he was out in the shop. When she heard a loud noise coming from the shop, she went out to see what it was. When she got out there he was lying on the floor. She went over to him calling his name. Dennis, Dennis, Are you alright! He didn't respond and he wasn't moving. She said she just stopped in her tracks and held her breath. She didn't see any blood, so that was a good sign she told Aggie. She said she knew she needed to check to see if he was alive. It took everything she had in her to reach down and check for a pulse.

As she was telling Aggie her story, Aggie could tell she was reliving it all over again. All Aggie could do is hold her hand and tell her they were here for them. Then she continued with her story. As she reached down to check for his pulse, his eyes opened up. She said "It scared the hell out of me!" Dennis asked her "What happened?" She told him, "I don't know, you were lying here when I came in. She told him "You scared the hell out of me." Again, I thought you were dead!" Dennis told her "I guess you're out of luck, I'm still here!" She hit him gently, and said "That's not funny!" Then she helped him up and gave him a big kiss and told him they were going to the hospital. Of course, he said no, but Frank's mom said she didn't give him a choice; she pushed him into the car.

She looked me in the eyes, as she told me, "He was fine, I almost didn't take him, and he was acting fine. All the way to the emergency room he complained how this is dumb and a waste of time. I just told him you can complain all you want, were going anyway!" Frank's mom stopped talking and asked Aggie to get her a cup of coffee. Aggie got up and poured them both a cup of coffee. Aggie sat back down in the chair and waited for Lola (Mom) to continue her story. As she looked into her coffee Aggie could tell she was lost in her thoughts. So Aggie touched her hand and said what happened next? She looked up in surprise, like she had forgotten that Aggie was there. She told Aggie "I'm sorry; I was just thinking how I will ever live without Dennis? All Aggie could do is get up and give her a big hug, and told her again they were all here for her. Aggie tried to get Lola's mind off of that thought, she asked her what happened next at the hospital.

She looked up at Aggie and said "We were standing at the emergency desk, when all of a sudden he couldn't breathe and he grabbed his chest. The receptionist grabbed the phone and called the code blue, and then jumped up and ran around the desk to help. Within seconds Dad was put into a wheelchair and taken into the back area. She smiled at Aggie and said "I didn't even know if I could go with him or not, but I'd be damned if I was staying behind. I guess it was okay, because no one tried to make me stop. I just had to stay out of the way." Aggie told her that must've been hard. Lola was looking into her coffee cup again. When she started to talk again, her replies surprised Aggie, "No, I knew I needed to let them do their jobs, I did mine job, and I got him there." Aggie patted her hand again and stood up and gave her another hug. Aggie told her I'm going to go check on the guys and she would be right back. Lola just smiled and thanked her and went back into looking into her coffee cup.

Aggie walked into the folk's bedroom, she could hear someone talking. She got a little excited; she thought maybe Frank's Dad was awake. But as she walked into the room, Dennis (Frank's dad) was still asleep. Frank was talking to him. He turned to her, and said "I know he can hear me!" She walked over to Frank and gave him a kiss and a hug. She didn't know what else to do or say.

Frank said "The doctor said he could pull through, but at his age he'll need to fight hard to make it. Then he looked at his dad and said, "I know my Dad can do it, he's a strong man, I know he will be fine. What's a little heart surgery to a man like him?" She had to agree with him, Aggie told Frank that he needs to go and be with his Mom. She would stay with his Dad. Yes, I'll talk to her, he didn't have to ask, and Aggie knew what he was thinking. He started to leave, then he turned to her and gave her a big kiss and a hug and said "I love you and thanks for being you!"

Aggie couldn't say anything as he turned and walked away. All she could do is smile! Aggie sat down next to Dad and started talking to him. She told him how the kids were doing and they wished they could be here. She talked about their trip up here and their plans to travel around the US. Maybe he and Mom could join them, once he gets better. It was unusual for Aggie to do all the talking. Dad was the talker, granted she can hold her own in a conversation. After a while Frank came back in and told Aggie, he had talked his Mom into lying down for a little while and that she was resting on the couch. When he left her, he thought she was asleep. "How is Dad doing?" Frank asked Aggie. Aggie told Frank, "The same." Frank told Aggie; "From my understanding Dad did have a double bypass surgery.

Everything went well. It was a good thing that Mom had taken him to the hospital when she did otherwise he wouldn't have made it."

Frank and Aggie were in his Dad's room talking when Styles, Frank's brother came in. Style smiled at them, and then he asked his dad, "Why are you still in bed, wake up and visit with us," just like that his Dad's eyes opened up, he looked a little confused but then he told Styles, "Why are you yelling at me?" We all started laughing, and hugging each other. Aggie went out and got Mom. Aggie thought she scared Frank's Mom because of the way she went running into the room. Aggie saw her face, and she told her that he was awake. Mom smiled and ran to the bedroom.

By then Dad was sitting up now. Mom went over to him and gave him a big kiss on the forehead and then the lips. He wasn't as confused anymore, the boys were both talking at the same time; asking how he felt, did he need anything. The boys really loved their dad. He told them, "I'm fine," Mom was pulling his blankets up and fixing his pillow. He looked at her and said, "Quit fussing over me, Woman!" Then dad got this big smile on his face and said "Well I made it, I guess you guys are stuck with me for a little while longer!" We all laughed and said, "No problem!"

For the next couple of weeks everyone helped around the folk's place. Dad wasn't allowed to do anything except to walk and do his breathing exercises. Styles had to leave and get back to his research ship. He called every night to see how things were going. The grandkids, nephews, nieces all came by to see him and to check on him.

One evening they were having dinner, when Frank's Dad asked them, "When are you leaving, don't you have someplace else to go?" We were surprised by his question. Then Mom spoke up and said "What he's trying to say is, he's fine and its okay for you guys to leave us alone, we'll be fine." They laughed and told them that they have been talking about heading up to Oregon and then Washington later on this month. Then Frank said "If your okay old man, I guess we will head out on Wednesday. Dad told him "Go enjoy life as much as you can, while you can!" Frank made sure someone came over to do the yard work and help his Mom out. Of course, his family, cousins, uncles and aunts and all their other friends that were around them would be there to check on them too.

Frank and Aggie loaded up their RV and said their goodbyes on Tuesday. The next day as they drove off waving at Mom and Dad it was hard to leave them, but she didn't think they needed them around anymore.

Chapter 3

Florence, OR

Frank and Agatha are heading up to Oregon; they planned on stopping along the coastline. Their plans are to do a little fishing and rock hounding as they went on their new adventures. They were going through Oregon, Washington, Idaho, and then across Arizona, and back to Texas, but that could change.

Frank called and talked to his parents today and got the good news that his Dad received a clean bill of health from the doctor. Aggie couldn't help thinking; she was glad that Frank goes in for his yearly checkups. They called the kids to let them know later on that night and they told them they are going to try to join them in a couple of months.

They both felt it is weird not having a plan, but they both agreed it was time to go with the flow. Aggie knew it was driving Frank nuts, but Aggie enjoyed not knowing what the plans were and where they would end up next. That's what makes an adventure!

The decision-maker will be a quarter that they had chosen to flip. They even had a place on the dash board, for it. They will flip the quarter to decide whether to go north or south or west or east. They planned on staying in one location for at least three weeks and explore the area around where they were.

Their first stop is Florence, Oregon. Aggie loved going to the visitor center and getting the history of the area. She always wanted to add the information to her journal. So with that said, here is the history of Florence. "Florence is located on the Oregon Coast at the mouth of the Siuslaw River. Florence is approximately midway between the other major central Oregon coastal cities of Newport and Coos Bay."

The history of "Florence was originally inhabited by the Siuslaw Indians, whose name to this day is shared by the impressive river that flows through the country where these Native Americans once lived. Europeans first began traversing this region during the Golden Age of Exploration, when Spanish galleons sailed off the coast, charting the territory. Years later, on his northwest voyage, the famous English seaman Captain Cook explored the Oregon coastline, giving names to many present day landmarks, such as Cape Foulweather."

"In the second half of the 19th century, Anglo-Americans permanently settled the area that would become Florence. This rugged frontier community depended on the logging and fishing trades for its economic survival. The town hit a landmark population of 300 in the year 1900, a year when it was proud to boast a lumber mill, two general stores, two canneries, a saloon, and a weekly newspaper. The town's vital link across the Siuslaw River was provided by ferry boats until 1936, when the picturesque Siuslaw River Bridge was completed. The ferries were soon made obsolete, as the automobile growth continued." There is a lot of history in this town.

As soon as Frank and Aggie arrived at their campsite, it was outside of Florence, it started to rain. It was raining so hard you couldn't go two feet forward, without getting soaking wet. Aggie was glad they have an RV instead of a tent to stay in. Some of the people around them that had tents looked miserable; others acted like it wasn't a big deal that it was just raining out!

They had covered their area with tarps this way the tents were kind of connected. It looked like everything was pretty much covered accept for the fire pit. It sounded like they had a great time last night. They could hear their neighbors' music and laughter as they settled in for the night. Tomorrow they will be heading over to Frank's aunt and uncle house, and staying on their property in Florence.

When he was 17 years old, his family had a family reunion outside of Florence, Oregon. His Uncle Harold had been to his parent's house earlier that year, and promised them a nice time if they came to visit them.

One of the biggest highlights of that weekend was his Uncle taking each of them up in his airplane. No one in the family had ever flown before in his family, and really didn't what to be the first one. But Frank had no problem volunteering to go up first, he was so enthusiastic about going up, his Uncle Harold told him to hop in.

Uncle Harold had a small air coupe, it could only carry two people, and it had a single engine. They are a little difficult to get in if you are not very athletic, or in good shape. There is no regular door that normally is on most planes. Instead, the roof on each side folds over and there is a high step to jump up on. But that didn't faze Frank; it wasn't difficult when he was a 17 year old boy. He just put one hand on the open top and found a good solid spot for his other hand and jumped in. Harold turned to Frank to explain the best way to enter the plane; but Frank had already bounced up into the air and placed his self into the co-pilot seat. Harold told Frank, "Well that is the way to climb in; most people break their backs trying to climb in the first time."

Uncle Harold fired up the air coupe, the motor sounded like a lawn motor. Harold called on his radio to get clearance to take off, he got the approval. A couple minutes later they were speeding down the one little runway of the Florence Air field. Suddenly they were up in the air; they headed out over the sand dunes and the nearby beach. Frank still remembers how cool it was to be up in the air, and how everything looked so different and small.

Later that day, after everyone in the family had a turn riding in the plane, they all had lunch. Hot dogs all around! Next we all went to the sand dunes, it is one of the bigger attractions they have in Florence. The dune buggies were made from some old jalopies, with padded bench seats. Each one held five to six people, and each one had a roll bar on it. There was a driver in each of them and they would take you out into the dunes and do some leaps, and tricky turns. It reminded Frank of his favorite show "Rat Patrol." It was one of the best weekends he ever had. Frank's Uncle Harold doesn't fly anymore, but they are having a Fourth of July BBQ. Frank was looking forward to seeing everyone.

When they arrived at Frank's Uncles house there were tents set up in one area and in another area had RVs. They assumed that they should park with the rest of the RVs. As they backed in the RV, everyone started coming out of their rigs and tents to welcome them. Aggie looked at Frank and

20

asked him, "Do you know all of these people?" All Frank did was smile and said, "Maybe, when they were much younger!"

There was family from all parts of Oregon. They introduced themselves to Frank and Aggie. Aggie felt funny because she had long pants and a light jacket on, so did Frank. Everyone else had shorts and tank tops. The tempture was in the 60's, and they told them this is our summer weather. If it gets over 55, we wear shorts.

Uncle Harold and Aunt Mary had seven kids, and 25 grandkids, and four great grandkids. There were a lot of people there when Frank and Aggie arrived, but as the day moved on, more arrived.

There was a main fire pit, everyone was asked to bring fire wood. Some of the people had a truck load of fire wood. Someone had cut long sticks for cooking hot dogs and marshmallows. There was a variety of games set up for the kids and adults to play. There was horseshoes, badminton, volleyball and of course football.

The older people pulled out their music instruments and started playing some old favorite songs. This of course ended up with people dancing from all ages. Everyone was having a great time. Frank and Agatha enjoyed meeting all of Frank's cousins. Frank had told Agatha the last time he saw most of these people they were it in their teens. Now they're all in their 50s and 60s and have families of their own. It was pretty late by the time that they headed towards their RV. It didn't take them long to go to sleep.

Apparently, Frank had become a little overcome, because he had a dream that a lot of very old people were crowding around him. He started to run; he didn't stop till he got to a cliff. He turned and they were yelling, "Come on Frank it's time, its time! They kept crowding him. Just about that time, an old guy grabbed him, and Frank woke up! Aggie was shaking him and was saying Frank come on get up! He was glad it was just a dream. He decided he wouldn't tell Aggie about the dream. There was no point in upsetting her. He had no clue what it met and hoped he never had that dream again.

When the dogs (the girls) came out of the RV, they were ready to go on their walk. Frank and Aggie were really surprised to see all of the dogs that were there big or small and they seem to all be getting along. They had an area roped off, an area for the dogs to play in and do whatever else they needed to do.

Uncle Harold only requested everybody to pick up after their dogs. Frank and Agatha walked over to the dog park and let the dogs run for a little while. Needless to say, there was a lot of smelling each other. Susi didn't like one of the dogs, so we kept them apart. The fact the dog was three times her size really didn't matter to her.

It was time for breakfast, you could smell the bacon. It was being cooked over the open fire pit, so the smell was just riding on the air. Frank thought to himself what a great smell. It was one of the things he missed most on the island. They decided it was time to walk over to the fire pit and see if they could help with anything. If they happen to get a couple of pieces of bacon in the process that would be ok by them.

Lucky for them, the buffet was already set up and everything was cooked. All they had to do is load up their plates and find a place to sit. Aggie thought how great this was, she didn't have to do anything except enjoy herself. Frank and Aggie had agreed before they started traveling, that she would do the work inside of the RV and Frank would do everything outside. Lucky for Aggie she didn't have to do any cooking here. Once the rig was set up there really wasn't much for Frank to do either, except if there was a dump site here. Otherwise, they would just wait and dump the sewage later.

After breakfast everyone headed over to the sand dunes again. Some of the family needed to rent the dune buggies they needed. Uncle Harold's property ran along the coast line. It was connected to a business that rented dune buggies. Six of the cousins had their own dune buggies, the rest of the group had to rent or connect up with other family members. It took a little bit to get everyone set up, but when everyone was all set up there were 15 buggies. What a site seeing all fifteen buggies lined up and taking off across the dunes.

It was wild seeing all those buggies flying over the dunes. A few of them just drove on the beach or drove really slow over the dunes. At one time they lined up six of the buggies and had a race down the beach. Crazy Joe won every event. He jumped higher, farther and went faster than anyone else. Well to be fair he did own his buggies and did racing events around the country. Cousin Joe (Crazy Joe) was the crazy one, but in their family, he was also the most interesting one. He didn't have many teeth and he had grey long curly hair, which he kept in a pony tail. He always had a cigar in his mouth or in his hand. The funny thing is he never lit it. He wore an old cowboy hat; he said he got it for a gift on his fifteenth birthday from his Dad. Joe is around 55 years old; his hat looked just as old! When Aggie asked him how old he was, he would give an off the wall line like; Older then dirt, but younger than a rock. Aggie had no idea what that meant. Aggie guessed he was around 55, or around there anyway.

He took a liking to Aggie and wanted her to go for a ride with him. She would only go if Frank went with her, she felt weird around Joe. The way he looked at her, how every time she would go somewhere he would be right there. He really didn't say much to her, but every time Aggie looked around there he was staring at her. She pulled Frank close to her, and asked him, "Have you noticed how Crazy Joe, is following me around?" Frank said he had, he wasn't sure how to take it, and he didn't want to start any trouble. Frank put his arm around Aggie and walked over to a crowd of people, thinking maybe they would lose Joe. But that didn't stop Joe, he just followed behind them. As the evening came, everyone started getting the fire started and the BBQ going. It was pot luck; there was lots of food, four types of potatoes salad, devil eggs, bake beans and three or four other types of beans. Some of the dishes that was on the table, Aggie was not sure what they even were. But Frank and she tried them anyway. A couple of the dishes Frank and Aggie couldn't decide what they were and didn't what to know. After Frank and Aggie loaded up their plates, they went over to sit down, there was Joe again.

When they finished dinner, they got up and headed over to the volleyball game. Frank couldn't stand it anymore, so he confronted Joe. Frank turned around and asked Joe why are you following my wife around? Joe just smiled and said, "She reminds me of my mother, I haven't seen her for a long time. She left my Dad, and took my older sister, she was three, and I was two at the time. I don't remember much about them. But my Aunt used to show me pictures and talk about my mother and older sister. His Aunt told him, she had lost touch with her after a few years, and she didn't know what happened to them. I'm sorry if I upset you guys." He started to get tears in his eyes. Aggie couldn't help it and gave him a hug and consoled him. Frank felt bad and patted Joe on back and told him, "Come on let's go play volleyball." He agreed and they all headed over to the game, arm and arm.

They all joined into the game, Joe was pretty good at it, and they even won a couple of the games. After three games, they all had enough and headed over to get a beer. They sat around the fire pit talking to other family member. When Aggie turned to ask Joe a question he wasn't there. Joe had disappeared, the next time Aggie turned around he was back. He had a banjo in his hand, it looked pretty old and it looked like it had been used a lot. Joe told them, it was his Dads. He loved to play it at family events and anywhere else that he could. Aggie asked Joe, "Do you play?" Joe replied, "Yes, but not as good as my Dad." Frank said, "Why don't you play us something?" It didn't take much encouragement to get him to play. Next thing you know other family members pulled out their instruments, and joined in with Joe's banjo playing.

Frank and Aggie looked at each other, Frank turned to Aggie, and told her, "I guess we'll have to learn an instrument, if we are goanna hang out with our families." There is nothing like live music to get things going at a family reunion. Even the teenagers joined in. In the beginning they acted like it was nothing they wanted to join in on. But next thing you know, they would be dancing and laughing at the songs. You could tell Joe loved playing his banjo. Before the night was over, Joe was playing the guitar and even some bongo. Frank had the biggest smile on his face and his foot was tapping along with the music. They were playing songs that Frank and Agatha have never heard before such as: Dark town Strutters ball, For me and my gal, Beautiful brown eyes, Beer Barrel Polka, but they also played some old greats like: Irish eyes are smiling, Bill Bailey, Irene good night, Oh Johnny and the list just goes on and on.

With the big bonfire and all of the dancing around the fire, it was a wonderful night. But finally Frank and Agatha had to say their good nights and head back to Penelope (their RV). As always they had to name their rig (RV), and this rig was called Penelope, she was a real sweetheart. Frank and Aggie did a little remodeling so they would have more space. After living on Rosland Island, they knew how to put space to good use.

CHAPTER 4

Pacific City and the Tillamook Area

The next morning, or should I say late morning they packed up their Rig and headed out. By the time they left it was 11 o'clock. It was about two hours later than they originally planned, but they are retired! They didn't really have to worry about getting someplace in a hurry. The plans were to head over to Pacific City, Oregon and spend some time in that area. They had heard the coast line was beautiful and they could drive up Hwy 101 and see the ocean most of the time. Aggie had to wonder if there were Merbeings living in the upper part of the Pacific Ocean. She had never heard of any, but that didn't mean there wasn't any. It was hard for Frank and Aggie not to think of Roslanders and the other Merbeings clans every time they saw the ocean. But there was so much more to see and do on land. This is the first time that they won't have any family around.

They decided this time not to connect the Jeep up to the rig. Aggie would take the lead with their Jeep. On their way to Pacific City, they wanted to stop and see the Sea Lion Caves. The Sea Lion Cave wasn't far from where they were at, only about ten miles. They had heard a lot about it. "The Sea Lion Cave is supposed to be a cave that had begun over 25 million years ago. It is as high as a twelve story building and stretches the full length of a football field." This is where the Sea Lions made their home, according to the flyer Aggie had picked up at the visitor center. Frank and Aggie always stopped at visitor center when they entered a new state or the site they were visiting.

It took a little bit to find a place to park the RV, but once they found a place, they were ready to visit the Sea Lions. As always Aggie had to read the information she found at the center. According to the information; these are Stellar Sea Lion; they are warm blooded mammals and live in the area. Its a little work to get down to the cave, but once your there you'll know it. The Sea Lions can be very loud and are laying everywhere on the rocks. The echo of theirs calls can be heard all around the cavern and up the stairs. As you start going down the stairs, it is kind of scarier, it sounds like a loud roar of some kind of sea monster. If you have never been there, you have no clue what it is. As you enter the cavern you know instantly, what it is, there are sea lions everywhere. Some of them were huge; the guide told the visitors that the males can weigh on to a ton. It reminded Frank and Aggie of the first time they saw the Merbeings in their cave, it wasn't as big as this cave, but it was pretty big. This was pretty amazing, watching the Sea Lions in their natural environment. The sea lions didn't care if humans were there or not. The guide told everyone to look across to the far wall of the cavern, where they would see an imprint of an Indian maiden. Sure enough they could see the maiden. "It was Amazing!"

After watching the Sea Lions, they got back on the road; they still had a couple hours to go, before reaching Pacific City. Aggie took the lead in the truck. This way if she saw anything interesting, she would call back to Frank on their CB and tell him what mile marker to watch out for. It didn't take long before Aggie spotted a large rest area. It was big enough for them to park Penelope and have something to eat.

The rest area was called Boiler Bay, just north of Depot Bay. It was kind of shaped like a W. It was up on the mountain range, there were cliffs on the ocean side. The middle of the W jetted out into the ocean, it was amazing. Frank and Aggie walked out to the edge, they were surprised how beautiful the Oregon Coast line is. Each side of the W had a diverse view of the coast line. As they looked down from the edge of the bluff, they could see for miles in each direction. In one direction, the beach was on one side that would go on for miles. There was no building or people on the beaches. Then they walked over to the other side of the view point, there was a drop off, which had a bay at the bottom. As the waves came crashing on to the rocks, the water would shoot up fifty to seventy-five feet at least. As they looked north they could see one outcrop after another. Each outcrop was topped with large pine trees and went as far as the eyes could see. They sure don't have this on the Texas coast! It was time to go to the next stop.

Frank and Agatha pulled into the campground outside of Cape Kiwanda. It was a nice size park; they had talked to the camp host of the park on the way in. She had told them that they could drive on the beach, in this area. There were a couple of roads that went right on to the beach. There were three different accesses one was at Cape Kiwanda, one was just a dirt road going down to the beach and the third one is right off of the road in Tierra Del Mar.

They set up camp and settled in for the night. The next morning they decided to drive over to the beach. It was cold and windy that morning, so they just parked the truck on the beach, and sat inside. They watched the ocean roll in and the people that were walking. Frank and Agatha love to people watch, it always amazed them the things people would do, and today was no different than any other day.

They were sitting in the truck watching when they saw a sedan driving onto the beach. The sedan did okay for a little while, but sure enough they got close to the water's edge and got stuck. Frank turned to Aggie, "Looks like we're going to get a show!" Aggie smiled, and told him, "Don't you think we should help?" Frank replied back, "Maybe, but it looks like they have help already." Frank pointed at a little truck, which had stopped to help them. Frank pointed out that, "The water isn't that close to them right now. There were already people out there trying to help them. If they need our help they will ask us."

At first the people in the car didn't act very worried about it. The kids were down by the water playing. But as time passed and the car was getting deeper and deeper into the sand. Also the water's edge was getting closer, with each wave the water got closer and closer.

At this point they had tried pushing, digging and even had a couple of little trucks trying to help pull them out, but to no avail. The trucks were just too small to get the job done.

One guy tried a rope and it broke, when it snapped it almost hit one of the people watching. Another guy tried to push it out but the truck front end was too high, and went right over the trunk of the car.

Aggie could see one of the little girls from the car and she assumed it was the little girl's mother walking toward them. Aggie got out of the truck and said Hi. They both replied Hi, and then started talking at the same time. The mother asked them if they had a rope or anything that would help them pull their car out. The mother pointed to a small truck next to their car and said, "He said he would pull our car out if we had something to pull it out for us." Frank told the mother, "I really don't think that little truck can pull your car out of the hole you have it in now." The mother and the little girl both put their hands up to their mouth and made a gasp of desperation. Frank put his hands up and said "It's ok, we'll help! We have tow ropes, and I'm pretty sure our truck can pull your car out."

By this time the water was coming up to the car tires. They all loaded up into Frank's truck. They pulled up to the front of the car, and Frank got out, and Aggie took the wheel. Frank took charge and hooked the tow rope to the sedan, and told everyone to get in the back and push, when Aggie starts to pull. Aggie pulled the truck out slowly until the rope was tight; Frank told everyone to push and called to Aggie, "Go for it!"

Aggie pushed down on the gas nice and slow, and had already put the truck into 4-wheel drive. At first the car wouldn't move, but she didn't give up. She looked into the rear view mirror and saw the six adults pushing on the back end of the car. To the right she saw the two little girls and their mother all praying. Aggie pushed the petal down again and gave it a little more gas, the car still didn't move. Now the water was going underneath the car. Frank told everyone to push the car back and forward until it broke loose. Aggie tried it again, this time giving it a little more gas; and then gave it all the truck could do. The sedan followed her out of the hole. She pulled the car to hard ground, there was cheering and clapping. The family that owned the car ran over to the car and loaded up and took off. Not a word, no thanks or a wave good-bye.

Aggie was a little upset, she told Frank, "They could have at least said thank you." Frank said, "I'm sure they were so happy to save their car, all they wanted to do is get off the beach. Besides, we didn't do it for the thank you! Aggie replied, "Maybe they were upset that we didn't help them sooner! We could have helped sooner." Frank smiled, "Could be, but I bet they'll never drive their car on the beach again!"

By now it was past dinner time; they were glad they had set up camp before going down to the beach. It had been a long day so they crawled into bed and did a little reading, and then it was lights out.

The next couple of days they explored the little towns in the area. They couldn't believe how many small towns were on the Oregon coast. In Texas you could go for miles and never see a town or a car.

Here they have towns inside of towns. Pacific City is the main one, but it is connected to Cape Kiwanda on the beach side, and then there is a small town on the edge on the other side of Pacific City. There are two rivers; one goes through Pacific City the Nestucca River. The other river is called Little Nestucca River; it's more of a creek. The valley is named Nestucca; other towns in the valley are Cloverdale, Hebo, Beaver and Oretown.

It's been cold and rainy for the last week. The weather man had said on the news that it was going to be sunny tomorrow. When Frank and Aggie woke up, they could see the blue sky. They both said at the same time, "Let's go to the beach! Agreed! They loaded the truck with a couple of chairs, ice chest and of course the girls. Then off to the beach for a quiet day, just enjoying the beach and watching the people go by.

They settled in next to the hillside so they would be out of the way of traffic. First thing they did is take the dogs for a walk on the beach. It was a beautiful day, there was no wind, and the sun was shining bright. The wind did start to pick up after awhile, they moved to the other side of the truck, to block the wind. As they settled into the chairs, they saw a small white truck driving onto the beach. Pretty soon the little truck was speeding down the beach like it was a freeway, then he would turn and do cookies, some people call them donuts. He would go around and around in a circle two or three times and then he would take off down the beach and do it again and again. Then he turned around and came back and did it all over again. It was quite a show! Who needs television?

When the white truck finally left, the next show arrived. It was a blue truck this time. They pulled close to the water's edge, and let three little dogs out. The dogs looked like miniature Dobermans. One stayed right by the truck and the other two ran in Frank and Aggie direction. On their way the two little dogs were checking everything out, as they were running toward Frank and Aggie. Then they turned and ran to the grass line.

In the meantime the people in the blue truck were enjoying a beer. The reason that Frank and Aggie knew this is because the driver tossed the empty beer can into the back of his truck. All of a sudden the blue truck took off down the beach leaving two of the dogs behind. As Aggie was watching the two dogs, they didn't act like they saw their owner leave. But then she saw both the dogs look in the direction of where the truck should have been. Then the dogs acted like they just realized that their owners were gone.

Both of the dogs took off running where the truck should have been. The little black one smelled around a little, and then took off at a full run towards the direction that the truck had gone. The Brown dog was still looking and smelling, and then it notices the black one was gone too. It was trying to figure out what was going on. But to no avail. Aggie called the dog, but he didn't want anything to do with her.

In the meantime the black dog was chasing after the blue truck. Aggies saw the blue truck stop and turn around. About that time the black dog was up to them. They opened the door and the dog jumped into their truck. The blue truck started back towards Aggie, she guessed that they must have realized they had forgotten their dogs. The little brown dog was still confused, it kept running in circles. Aggie couldn't tell if the people in the blue truck could see the brown dog or not. She started waving her arms and pointing at their dog. They finally spotted their dog and drove over to it, and the door flew open and the dog jumped in. They turned around and waved at Aggie as they drove off. Another happy ending on the beach.

Aggie walk back to Frank and sat down. Frank told Aggie, "I can't believe they forgot their dogs!" She had to agree, "At least they came back for them!" Frank smiled at her and reminded her of the little dog they had found at the beach last year at his parents' house. Aggie said, "At least we didn't have to keep their dogs!"

It settled down for a little while on the beach, when Frank spotted something moving on the beach. It was small, and it was moving against the wind. He pointed it out to Aggie and said, "I think it's a mouse! Aggie responded, "It can't be, it must be a leaf. Frank told her if it was a leaf it wouldn't be going against the wind. They couldn't stand it any longer and got up to check it out. As they got closer to whatever it was, it would move. Sure enough it was a mouse to be more specific, it was a Skew. It was a little guy; about 2 inches long not including the tail. It looked out of place; normally mice don't hang out on the beach. It would try to hide beside a pile of sand, and then it would take off. It was running towards the water and some seagulls were in that direction, and disappeared. Aggie told Frank, "Maybe it's the Seagulls pet." Frank laughed and said you never know! About that time the white truck had returned and was flying down the beach again, doing his show again. "They both stated at the same time "Great!"

Frank asked Aggie, "Are you ready to go back to the RV? She agreed and they loaded up their things into the truck and then went back to Penelope. They hung out at the RV and got a fire started. Then of course they had to get out the cards and play a couple of hands of Spite and Malice. They started planning for the next day, they had a list of things that they wanted to do. They wanted to go to the Pioneer Museum, the Cheese Factory in Tillamook and a few other places in that area. It was always interesting talking to the other RVer's; they would get ideas where to go around the area.

The next morning they got up early and headed towards Tillamook. They had heard about a waterfall which was called Munson Falls. They decided that they would stop at the Munson Falls first; it was on the way to Tillamook anyway. They almost missed the turn off; all it had was a small brown sign, showing where it was at.

The parking area was small; there is no way a RV of any type could have gotten in there. It was a little hike into the forest, about a quarter of a mile, but it was worth every step. The woods were beautiful; it was all overgrown and there was mostly Western Red Cedar and Spruce trees. It looked like man hasn't touched it in hundreds of years. It looked a lot like a rain forest. As they got closer to the waterfall you could hear the loud roar of the waterfall. As they got closer they could see bits and pieces of the waterfall. As they went over the top of the hill, there was the waterfall in all of its glory.

From what Frank and Agatha understood this was one of the largest waterfalls in Oregon and one of the best-kept secrets in the state. It is a spectacular view; it is an impressive waterfall with a stunning 266 foot drop, making it one of the Oregon's largest falls and certainly one of the most beautiful. It is kept in its natural state when a tree falls across it, it will stay there, until Mother Nature removes it. Aggie took lots of pictures, and told Frank she wished the kids could see this. They both missed not having their kids and grandkids with them.

The next stop was the Air Museum; it was also amazing with all of the history that was packed into one hanger. The hanger was originally used for blimps; it could house 3 to 4 of them at a time. There were originally two of these hangars, but one was being used as a storage area for hay. When the hay caught on fire and burned down the blimp hangar. The second one was turned into a museum where they kept a variety of planes, cars and even a few blimps. There was so much to see, Frank really enjoyed looking at all the old Army equipment and the old planes. There was a lot to see, but Aggie couldn't help thinking to herself, it sure is cold in here. She couldn't wait to leave; it was just too cold in there!

Inside the hangar, there was a nice little hamburger café. It was located in the front area, where they also had a gift shop. Agatha and Frank stopped there and had their lunch after finishing checking everything out in the Museum. The next stop was going to be the Pioneer Museum in Tillamook, which has been there since 1935. Of course, Agatha loves all the history and would always want to go to the different museums in the area. Frank loved the military part of the museum.

Museums were one of their favorite things to do in each of the cities that they went to. As they walked around the Pioneer Museum it was amazing to see all the different types of things they had. They had a geological records, military room, natural history dioramas, old-time country kitchen, steam logging donkey and a Victoria room. There was so much, much more to see. The museums must have had hundreds of stuffed animals, from all over the world. They were all on display for people to see what they really look like. The lady at the front desk had told Frank and Agatha about a hiking trail, outside of the city. They might enjoy going for a walk there, it was called Kilchis Point Trail, in Bay City.

According to the flier they had, "Kilchis point was the site of one of the largest Native American villages on the northern Oregon coast. The site was also one of the first pioneer settlements in what would eventually become Tillamook County. It is a reserve of 200 acre of natural beauty."

Frank and Aggie headed off down one of the trails, according to the map; it was about a two mile walk. As they walked along the trail, every so often there would be a little sign that would give them information about the area that they were walking through. According to one of the signs, the villages were comprised of plank houses and long boats. Log houses were similar to the ones used by other Oregon tribes. Up to three related families would live in one of the houses, which had two or more fireplaces in the center of the building. Arranged along the walls were matting separating the bedrooms from the main living area.

Frank and Aggie would stop at each of the little signs and read the information. Agatha could visualize the squaws and the children gathering the long beach grass, which was long and had sharp edges, they would use it to make their baskets and bedding. They would dry the beach grass out and make it into what every type of basket they needed, or other items that could be used around the village. It wasn't hard to see how the villagers would thrive in this area. There is wildlife and even different fruits and berries that were wild in the area, at that time and still there today.

As Frank and Agatha followed the path, there were a few areas that were a little rough to get around. But it didn't stop them from making it to the bay. There were a variety of birds: blue herrings, hawks, ducks, some type of white bird and even an owl. It was so peaceful and quiet there that they stood and watched the birds as they flew from one area to another to find food.

After they completed the trail, they headed back to the car. When they got back to the car, Frank couldn't help it, and asked Aggie. "Did you notice each couple that we passed on the trail was very friendly? It is funny how when you're on a hike, how people act different, they are so much friendlier. More than likely, if you ran into that same person in the city, they wouldn't give you the time of day. It happens even more so, when you have dogs." Aggie couldn't help but wonder why that is.

They loaded up the girls in the car, and headed home. Aggie couldn't help think that the girls will sleep well tonight, because they sure had a great day, running around the park.

They had heard that it was going to be nice tomorrow; so they decided to just enjoy the beach tomorrow. They all loaded up the next afternoon and drove down to the beach.

Aggie really loved the idea of driving on the beach. That way they could take their chairs, ice chest and whatever else they wanted to set up. She remembers the days when they could carry everything on their backs.

After setting everything up on the beach, they headed down the coast line with the girls. It was mid afternoon on a Wednesday, so there weren't a lot of people out, which was always nice. With no one around they could let the girls run free. Susi ran and barked and Sheba just barked at Susi for running and barking. After awhile they settle down and just ran and checked out everything on the beach.

As they walked down the beach they saw a couple coming toward them. It looked like they had two little dogs too. As the couple got closer Aggie put the girls on their leash just in case there was a problem. They could see the couple doing the same thing. Better safe than sorry, Aggie thought to herself.

As the couple got nearer they said, "Hello and asked how things were going? Aggie replied, "Great, what a beautiful day!" Aggie then asked if their dogs were friendly, they replied yes! It didn't take long for the dogs to check each other out. The dogs acted like they knew each other, and started to play with each other. They took all the dogs off their leashes and they ran off like little kids.

Aggie introduced herself and Frank, the couple introduced themselves as Larie' and Dean. After a few minutes Larie' asked Aggie and Frank, "Where are you from? It sounds like you're from the south." Aggie told her that they lived in Houston, TX. Aggie asked Larie' where they were from, Larie' told her from Hillsboro, OR, it's about sixty miles from here.

One thing led to another, and Aggie was telling them how Frank's father had a heart attack earlier this year. It made them stop and think about what they wanted to do with the rest of their lives. They have always wanted to explore the

US, so they decided it was time do some exploring. Traveling the good old USA! Larie' had told them that they were just starting to go full time, and they plan on heading to Texas too.

Dean and Frank hit it off as well, they were both retired army, and about the same age. They all had been walking while they were visiting with each other, and they ended up back at Frank and Aggies's Jeep.

They talked for a little while longer before heading back home. By then it was starting to get a little windy, so it was time to collect up their dogs, and say their good-byes. The dogs acted a little upset. Aggies's girls wouldn't get into the Jeep, and Larie's dogs wouldn't follow them either. Aggie guessed the dogs wanted to hang out with their new friends; they finally had someone to play with. Frank picked the girls up and put them into the Jeep, and Dean put the leashes on their dogs, and started down the beach.

Larie' and Dean walked down the beach and then disappeared into the woods. Frank and Aggie were just sitting in their Jeep, watching the ocean for a little while longer. Aggie told Frank, "Larie' was telling me about all these cool places to see not far from here. We should go there tomorrow; it's on the way to Tillamook. Frank agreed and turned on the radio and handed Aggie a bottle of water and said, "Cheers!"

The next day Aggie was ready to go, she likes to check out new places. They decided to leave the girls at home this time, so they could stop and have lunch at a place Dean had told Frank about.

Larie' had told them to take the road north and follow the "Three Capes Scenic Route" signs. It'll take you to Cape Lookout State Park, Cape Meares Light house, and the Octopus tree. If you follow the road it would take you to Tillamook, but it wasn't part of their plan today.

They pulled into the Cape Meares parking lot; it was nearly empty, mostly because it was pretty early, 7:00 a.m. They arrived early enough to almost have the place to themselves. There were two other cars there. As they parked they could see the ocean, to the right they saw an overlook that they could go stand on if they wanted. Of course, they did! They walked onto the overlook; they could see over the cliff edge, there were two little rock islands coming out of the ocean. It was beautiful. According to the sign the cliffs were used by Murre and Puffin birds and the seals used the rocks below.

Cape Meares lighthouse wasn't active anymore, it was active from the 1890s and in 1963 it was replaced with an automated beacon. Aggie wasn't sure what that meant; she assumed it meant that it didn't have to be manual anymore.

As they walked down the paved pathway toward the lighthouse, they could see the top of the lighthouse. It looked like a large red candy inside a glass tube. Aggie told Frank, I would hate to be walking down this path and have the light come on. Frank agreed it would be blind you!

The view was wonderful along the path; there were break area along the pathway so people could look over the cliff onto the crashing surf hundreds of feet below. They arrived at the lighthouse, it was a smaller lighthouse then the other ones they had seen earlier, and it stood on the cliff edge. It had a little white building connected to the side of the lighthouse. Larie had told her the little build was a museum at one time, but was closed now.

They had seen lighthouses all along the Oregon Coast line, but hadn't stopped at any of them. According to the map on the wall at Cape Meares, there are nine lighthouses; only five are still being used in its original set up.

The next stop was the Octopus tree, the good news was the tree was in the same area, it was just a short walk from the parking lot. As they walked up the path, the forest was quite, as they could hear the ocean coming through the woods. The Octopus tree was incredible, it was a Selka Spruce. According to the sign, "It is not known what caused the shape of the tree. It is 52 feet in circumference and has no central trunk. It is estimated to be 250 to 300 years old." Frank told Aggie, "The name says it all; it does look like an Octopus!"

It was time to head home and get ready for the next day travel. It was time to go in land, this was the first nice day they had had in a while. It had been raining off and on for the last week and it kept getting cooler and cooler. They were Texans and they like the heat and the sun!

That evening as they watched the news the weather forecasts showed it was suppose to be much warmer in land, which was fine with them. Aggie had a cousin that lived in Bend, Oregon. Her name was Wanda, and her husband's name was Earl. They had lived in the area for over 40 years; it would be great to see them again. It had been a good fifteen years since they have seen each other. Aggie told Frank he should call Wanda in the morning to see if they were going to be around and find out where would be a good place to set up camp.

With the next adventure figured out, it was time to hit the sack. They had picked up everything outside the day before, because there was going to be a big storm coming in that night and they didn't want to have to deal with loading up the rain. Otherwise, they would have to deal with all the wet items. That was never any fun!

Well the weatherman was right! The storm came in full blast, it had poured down all night. As Aggie lay in bed, she could hear the rain coming down on Penelope. It sounded like they had parked under a waterfall. Then the wind would blow, she could hear the large pine trees blowing in the wind, it was hard to tell if it was the trees or ocean. Of course, the girls were in bed with them, they didn't like the storm at all.

She couldn't help but think of Rosland Island and the storms they used to watch there. She missed the lightning storms on the island. It always looked like the ocean and the sky were fighting with each other. The whole sky was lit up; there was only the light from the storm. The lighting was never the same, each time it had a different design, and to make sure you were paying attention, the thunder would explode, crack and BOOM! The girls would jump up and whimper and try to get under the covers. It was going to be a long night.

The storm that Aggie was listening to tonight was a pup compared to the ones on the island. She was glad that they had packed everything up, earlier that day. As she felt asleep with both of the girls as close as they could get to her, she thought to herself, "It's going to be a long day tomorrow. It will be nice to have some sunny weather again!

Earlier that week, they had found a shortcut that would cut off 25 miles of the trip.

Chapter 5

On the road again!

The next morning Frank and Aggie started moving around; Frank started finishing up the outside chores. Aggie took the girls for a short walk, while Frank disconnected the water, electric and got everything ready to go. Aggie had already packed up most of the items inside of the rig the night before. Even with doing a lot of the packing the day before, it still took an hour before they could leave. Of course it started to rain again.

Their plan was to go through Hebo, and take a back road they had discovered earlier during the week. When they had found the road earlier that week they, also discovered an old fort, it was called Fort Yamhill. It was an interesting place with a lot of history that started in 1700s. The Northwestern Native Americans such as the Yamhill Kalapuya had lived in this area for thousands of years. Everything changed when the arrival of the Spanish, British, French Canadians and Americans started exploring the area, they we're looking for gold, and furs.

According to the information board, "The settlers were afraid of the native people, they had the U.S. Army bring in forces. There were about 80 enlisted men and four officers, at the Yamhill fort. But their mission was unique, they were supposed to prevent violence rather than engage in battle. But by 1855 hostilities had grown so fierce that something had to be done to save the Native Americans. Indian Affairs and Oregon territory set up the Native Americans bill. In 1850 the Oregon Indian bill directing Native Americans onto reservations. The land law allowed the government to seize all non-reservation land and redistributed to settlers. By 1855 Western Oregon tribes and bands signed treaties with United States government, giving up their homeland in exchange for reservation life. In 1856 Fort Yamhill was established. According to the flyer that they had at the site, there was a lot of history there."

Agatha and Frank walked around the area. It had some beautiful trails; one trail led up to the top of the mountain. It went in between two hills; on one side was a magnificent view of the Grande Ronde Valley, to the northwest was the Yamhill River Valley, which ran from the south and then headed east. Aggie turned to Frank and said, "What a beautiful place, it so sad that there was so much violence at one time here. As they walked around the different buildings that were still left, it was mostly just rock foundations. They did have a map showing where everything was at one time; it was a very interesting place to visit. But it was time to head home, they had left the dogs behind, and didn't what them to be left to long in the RV alone.

The shortcut they had found earlier that week was a success. It saved them a good 26 miles plus about 45 minutes of time. They figured it was a four hour trip, so they should arrive in Bend around 2 o'clock. Not all things work out as planned.

The rain was so heavy they ended up making a wrong turn in Salem and had to go farther down the freeway. This caused them to add another hour of travel time and about 60 miles extra to the trip. They were hoping to out run the storm but it followed them all the way to Salem.

As they turned onto Highway 20 and started heading up the mountain range the storm had caught up to them again. They decided to stop and have lunch before heading up the mountain; they figured they had another three hours to go, so they wanted to get some food and rest. They stopped in Brownsville at a truck stop, to get lunch.

They had read a flyer at the table, it had information about Brownsville. As usual Aggie had to write down some of the information about the town; there is a lot of history in this area. This is only a little bit of the information she had found. "Brownsville, is one of Oregon's earliest settlements, in 1846 is when a group of families including the Kirks, Browns and Blakely's arrived.

In 1858, both North Brownsville and the town of Amelia developed as separate communities on the north side of the river. A dam was constructed three miles upriver, and a ditch (millrace) was dug to supply reliable water power for industry in the new towns. First a grist mill, then a woolen mill, sawmill, furniture factory, and tannery, were established on the north side of the river. The railroad came to town in 1880, and by 1884, North Brownsville had become a bustling manufacturing and trade center serving a population of 300, as well as travelers on the railroad and the Territorial Road.

In 1895, the north and south sides of the river consolidated as the City of Brownsville. In 1919, a fire destroyed many buildings in the downtown area, but the energetic trade's people conducted "business as usual" in tents and homes until the town could be rebuilt.

As Frank and Aggie was reading about Brownville, they discovered there was a rock museum. They decided to check out the Rock Castle. The Rock Castle was also called "The Living Rock" it is primarily made of concrete, local agates, petrified wood and flagstone. "It has been estimated that the massive building contains over 800 tons of rock, according to the information sheet they had at the museum."

The inside walls are decorated with lava shale, sandstone, obsidian, quartz and agate specimens. The pillar in the center of the building is in the shape of a tree. They call it the "Tree of Life," it stands two stories high, with branches that extend up to support the ceiling. "The tree was built with an outer layer of petrified wood. The core of the tree was lined with an assortment of crystals. Rocks were not only used in the construction of the studios, but were also placed throughout the building. Rocks, such as Iceland, spur and naterlite, were encased in jars and embedded within the walls."

As Frank and Aggie looked around they continued to find different things throughout the museum. They even had a piano that had come over the Oregon Trail. They talked to the granddaughter of the gentlemen that built it. She talked about how she would work on the house with him. She told them stories about how he did the different projects. It was all built by their own hands, no heavy equipment was used. Aggie enjoyed talking to her; she always loved hearing people's stories.

She told Aggie and Frank, "It is more than a castle made of stone and cement. It is a work of art, a wonderland of rock, art and history. There are some beautiful, one–of–a–kind woodcarvings. Pictures made of thin translucent pieces of rock collected and arranged in such a way that when lit from behind, the pictures become glowing illustrations. Also, there were some original life–size oil paintings of various species of bird and a large assortment of rocks." It is so amazing what the human race can come up with!

It was time to go, so they looked over the map again; to make sure they knew where they were going and that's when they discovered they had really went out of the way to go over to Bend.

They headed up the mountain, Frank was in the lead with the RV and Agatha was following behind in the truck. They only had a hundred and twelve miles go, to reach their next campsite. It should only take two hours to get there.

The sky was getting dark and the rain was coming down in buckets. As they climbed up the mountain, the weather broke, Frank could rest easier. It wasn't easy driving in the rain normally, but he also had one of the windshield wipers starting to fall apart. All Frank could do is hope the wiper would stay together, at least until they reached their new location.

Aggie was still following Frank, as she looked over to the side of the road, there were four large vultures having their dinner. All of a sudden they flew off; Aggie was surprised at how big they were. They had at least a six foot wingspan, and an ugly bald red head. The vultures in Texas weren't that big. She laughed to herself, as she guessed it was because there was more food here.

As they continued up the mountain, the bad weather returned. Frank had to slow down to 30 miles an hour. Then to top it off there was road construction. As they continued climbing up the mountain, they looked out over the edge and they could see for miles. What a view Aggie thought to herself. They had been told from other Texans, how beautiful and green Oregon is. But the rain was pretty much stopping them from seeing anything.

As they reached the summit, they were out of the weather long enough to see what they had heard about. They could see for miles and miles. Aggie radioed to Frank and told him, did you see the view? It is a beautiful sight. Frank replied back, he had, it is too bad there's not any place to pull off.

Frank and Aggie were glad they finally reached the summit, as they started heading down hill, their speed picked up. But before too long they started climbing again. All they could only think of, this is one high mountain! After awhile they came to another summit and they started down the mountain again. This time it was all downhill, after three hours on the mountain they finally came off on the east side of the mountain, and were heading into Sisters. Sister is a small town, but it was very busy, the traffic was back to back bumper. After they finally got through there, Aggie radio Frank and said, "Looks like a nice town, but it's to crowd for me. Frank agreed with her.

They only had sixty miles to go to reach their camp ground. They had left Pacific City at 9:00 and it was now 3:30! It has taken them a lot longer than they had planned. But the good news was the weather was a lot nicer on this side of the mountain range.

CHAPTER 6

Bend

Afterward, they drove through Bend, and headed toward La Pine. By 5:00pm they finally arrived at their new site. It was called Bend-Sunriver Campground. It was quite an interesting site and even featured a ghost town. Granite it wasn't a real one, but it was still interesting to look at. It had a little cemetery, a jail, grocery store, and many other little buildings. They also had a lot of rabbits everywhere they were all kinds of colors, and sizes.

It didn't take them long to find a place to set up camp. It was much bigger than the site in Pacific City. After Frank and Aggie settled in for three weeks, they started walking around the campground. When they found a nicer site not too far from where they were at. This site had more open space. They decided to move into it. So they went back to their site and broke down everything, and moved to the new site.

That evening they went over to Wanda and Earl's and visited with them. They agreed that they would go with them to visit Crater Lake National Park, later that week. Frank and Aggie have been trying to visit Crater Lake for years. But something always came up.

On their way back to camp, they stopped to get groceries. They loaded up the truck with their supplies and headed home. It was a short drive to the campground from the store, it was only 15 miles.

Frank told Aggie, "I'll bet the girls will be happy to see us. They decided to take a short cut home instead of taking Hwy 97, which is usually a very heavily traveled road. Aggie looked down at the gas tank gauge and saw they had a little over a quarter tank. They passed a gas station when Frank asked Aggie, "Do we need to get some gas?" Aggie replied back, "No, we have a quarter tank of gas and we are only going five miles, we'll pick some up tomorrow." By then they had passed the gas station. As they continued on their trip home, it seemed like any other time.

It was a dark night, the moon was out but it was only a half moon, it didn't give off much light. On each side of the road all there was, were dark woods. This particular evening as it turned out, they were pretty much alone on the drive. They were ever so watchful for deer to come bouncing out of the darkness. Frank could see their yellow eyes along the side of the road, in the tree line.

Everything seemed to be normal for the first 15 or 20 minutes. Frank and Agatha were talking about their day's adventures. How nice it was to see Wanda and Earl. As Frank was watching out the window it came to him that there should've been a fire station on the right side of the road by now. He brought it to Agatha's attention that it is taking a lot longer to get home; we should've already been there by now. Aggie agreed that it does seem like it is taking a lot longer, but it looks right. So they continued to drive on.

Frank is a good navigator; he kept a good watched out for any deer that might pop out of the darkness. He could see numerous deer on the side of the road, just at the edge of their headlights. But fortunately they stayed put, until after they had passed. But after about 15 more minutes he began to wonder why they had not yet seen the fire station. So he mentioned it to Agatha again that this isn't right. There really wasn't much that they could do so they continued on. They were on pins and needles waiting to see something that they recognized soon, but more miles passed by.

They couldn't see beyond the length and the edge of the headlights. They started talking about, should they turn around and go back to Highway 97, or continue on the road they are on. It didn't make sense to Agatha she was pretty sure that it was a straight shot from the gas station to the road they were taking to the RV campground.

They began to feel like they were in the twilight zone, nothing was making sense. But they decided to go ahead and drive into the darkness, waiting to spot the firehouse that they couldn't have missed.

Suddenly they saw a sign; it was a yellow information sign that read "Chain Up Area." Frank told Agatha "I don't remember seeing a chain up area sign on this road before." She agreed, and glanced down at the gas gauge, it was reading quarter tank, and on they drove. Aggie began to wonder where in the hell they were going. Frank kept suggesting that maybe they should turn around.

Agatha finally pulled the car over and asked Frank for her phone to get directions back to the campground from the

GPS. After waiting a little bit it showed a long blue road, from our location, taken us back by several large lakes. The fact that there were no large lakes by their campground had Agatha a little worried.

They continued to go up and down roads they hadn't heard of before. The GPS estimated their drive time at a little over an hour. They weren't sure how long the gas would hold up but decided to trust the GPS on the phone. They continued to follow the road. Lucky for them, most of the way that the phone had sent them was going downhill, saving gas at least. Hopefully it will be enough!

Three times they were given instructions to turn and each time they questioned if it was really the right turn. They would turn onto a road totally different from the one they were on, and each time they wondered if that was the right move. Each of the roads seemed to be getting dark as hell, and Frank could always see those eyes in the darkness. He thought to himself they look like demon eyes, just waiting to jump out into our path.

The first road they were on was a very well maintained highway, smooth payment and well marked. Then the GPS told them to turn left in 500 feet, so they did. The next road was old, worn from years of use and much more narrow. Then the GPS said continue for 7 miles and then turn left onto a State Forest Rd., #47. They traveled along for the 7 miles, until the GPS instructed them to turn right in 500 feet, onto a smaller dirt road.

This time the road was washboardie, gravel road, going off into the darkness, with forest on both sides. Just beyond the headlights there were more of the yellow eyes, looking back at them from the darkness.

Frank and Agatha couldn't help but think about what they had heard on the news earlier this year. It was about a family that had gotten lost using the GPS system. They had gotten lost in the Oregon Mountains following the direction of the GPS. They had thought they were taking a shortcut, but ended up stuck in a snow bank and nobody knew where they had gone. They were lost for a week when they were finally discovered. The mother and the baby were inside the car but the father was missing. He had gone to find help. They found him a couple weeks later down in the ravine dead.

Frank and Agatha were really hoping that the GPS was actually given the right directions. As they continue in the darkness, driving down a rugged Jeep trail. Nearly out of gas and wondering what would happen next. But they continued on, just as the road looked like it was going to get worse the GPS said, "Turn onto Century Drive in 500 feet!" They were relieved to read Century Drive, this is the road that they were originally were supposed to be on. After 80 miles they finally arrived on the right road. It turned out that Century Drive, not only runs by Three River Resort, but also continues to make a huge loop over Mount Bachelor and circling all the way back to Bend.

Agatha continued to watch the gauge as it got closer to the red mark. The good news was the road went downhill again, so it looked like they were going to make it. The problem was they may have enough gas to get to the campsite, but they may not have the gas to get back to a gas station. The closes gas station was five miles away from the campground. But that was a problem for tomorrow, they were happy to be home again.

The girls were happy to see them; they arrived home around 10 o'clock. The girls reminded them; they still had to take them out for a walk. The campground was so quiet and dark but it was a relief just to be home. Frank and Agatha talked about how they could have missed the road; it should have been just straight shot. All Frank could say, "It's the twilight zone!"

The next morning Agatha wanted to go to the hardware store to pick up some things, they wanted to set up the screen room. But the real reason for heading that way was to see where they made their mistake. After about 5 miles she turned right and went to the hardware store. It still didn't make sense to her, how she could miss that road. But on the way back home she realized that she had just missed the left turn, the night before. It was after the gas station, and then she should have taken a left on Century Drive. The mystery was solved! Agatha couldn't wait to get home to tell Frank she had solved the mystery.

As they were going on their daily walk, they discovered a better place to park the RV in the campground than where they were. Again they packed up everything and moved to the new site. It had a lot more space and areas for the dogs to walk. So for the next two days they set up camp and got everything squared away. On the third day the plan was to go to the Lava River Cave with Wanda and Earl.

It was one of the uncollapsed lava tubes in Oregon; it is 5466 feet long, which now was a cave. It is about 100,000 years ago this conduit carried lava of 2000 degrees Fahrenheit (1100 Celsius). It came from an onslaught to lower areas of the flanks of the Newberry volcano. The formation that they would be going into was the aftereffect of the lava draining out of it.

Frank and Aggie met Wanda and Earl at the Lava River Center at 10:00 am. Everyone was on time; they headed over to the office, and were issued flashlights for a small fee. The Ranger explained to them that there were 350 stair steps going down into the cave, and then another mile to the end of it. They all looked at each other and agreed to give it a try. The good news was if they wanted to turn around they could. The Ranger wasn't kidding about the stairs; at least they had a platform every twenty steps. Wanda turned to Aggie and said, "Well I guess we'll get our work out today." They all agreed!

They finally got to the cave itself, and started walking on a path that was made for people to walk on. As they walked along they could see ice on the roof, they had been told by the ranger that it never got any warmer than 42 degrees in the cave. They were all glad they had put on a warm jacket and had gloves. Earl was telling Frank, that their daughter and her friend use to find lava tubes and explore them. But now the National park service had taken over most of the tubes, or had blocked them off so no one could go into them.

As they walked along they continued to look around. After a while it was pretty much the same thing. Aggie suggested that they turn off their lights, so they did. Of course, they had done this in the other cavern they have been in before. They all turned off their flashlights, and sure enough it was just as dark as the other caves they have been in "Pitch Black!"

As they were getting close to the end, they could hear lots of noise coming from the far end of the cave. They looked at each other and said, "Kids!" Frank suggested that they should wait where they were at, because it was a wide space in the cave. Sure enough after a couple of minutes, the kids came pouring out of the darkness.

It was a whole class of kids on a field trip, all talking a mile a minute. Aggie asked a couple of them how they liked it, they just replied "Cool" Frank and Earl just looked at each other, and wondered where are all these kids were coming from.

There had seen a school bus in the parking lot, but really didn't think there would be that many kids, it was hard to believe that many people could fit into the cave. After about ten minutes the kids stopped coming out of the darkness. At one point Frank said, "We should turn off our flashlight, and jump out at the kids. They laughed and decided that wouldn't be a good idea. But how funny it would have been! This would be a great place to have a haunted cave.

After everyone passed by they decided it was time to head back. As they got closer to the opening you could see day light. The way the sunshine broke the darkness was beautiful, and warm. It was just a little bit of light, but with each step up you could see and feel the difference in the cave. It had been so cold in the cave, but as they climbed the staircase, it got warmer and warmer. It was wonderful to feel the warmth of the sun again, Aggie thought.

The couples said their good-byes in the parking lot, and agreed to go to Crater Lake National Park, later that week. As Frank and Aggie headed home, they decided to see where they had traveled last night, when they had gotten lost. They knew how to get to the first part of where they got lost, but they weren't sure about the rest of the trip.

As they headed up the mountain pass they requested directions to get back to their campsite. But all the GPS would do is told them to turn around and go back down the mountain. Neither one of them could understand why it wouldn't work this time, but it did work when they were really lost. They decided to go ahead and go up to Mt. Bachelor. It was quite the scenic view. The mountain could be seen standing tall from all directions. Agatha had to wonder if the mountains in this area were all volcanoes at one time or another. There was a resort area at the top of one of the mountains. It had lifts that would take people up to the top of the hill, but they decided they needed to get back to the girls.

As they were driving into the campground they saw a fawn and its mother grazing in the wooded area and to their delight there was actually twins. The deer's looked at them like they were no big threat and they continued to eat, but mom did keep a good eye on them.

Back at the RV, the girls were waiting for them, they could see they in the windshield window. Frank opened the door to the RV, and Susie jumped out of the RV with her leash in her mouth and was ready to go for a walk. Frank turned to Agatha and said, "I guess we'll be going for a walk now!" Agatha laughed and said, I guess so! So they put their leashes on Susie and Sheba and headed down the road for a walk. The next couple of days they hung around camp and worked on the RV maintenance and did some cleaning inside. It was nice just to hang around and do some reading and watch a little TV for a change, Agatha thought.

They had made plans with Wanda and Earl to meet them at the RV and they would all take the Jeep up to Crater Lake. They showed up at 10 o'clock on the dot. Agatha had made a picnic lunch for everyone and off they went on to a new adventure. This time the girls (the dogs) were going to go with them. It only took an hour and a half to get to Crater Lake from their campground.

As they entered the National Park, their first stop was the North Junction where they had to decide if they wanted to go left or right. Either way the road led them around the rim of the massive crater. Which was filled with the deepest blue water, they have seen in a while. They had decided to go left for no reason but just to do it. Many of the different things at the park were closed for the winter. Agatha just told Frank they would just have to come back again in the summertime to take the tour boat and do some hiking. As they pulled into their first view point of Crater Lake it was astonishing.

Aggie and Wanda looked at the map of Crater Lake, and found the information about each turn off. There were six overlooks; each had different positions on the lake, and a little information board with a story to tell. This overlook was called Discovery Point; this is where John Hillman first discovered the lake in 1853. Aggie could relate to what he must have felt, as this was her first time seeing the lake too. He named it Deep Blue Lake; as far as Aggie was concerned he named it right.

They all unloaded from the car and stood at the Discovery Point Overlook. As they looked over the rim the dark blue water it glittered, as the sun danced on the water. In the distance they could see a little island. According to the map that they received from the ranger station, it was called Wizard Island. It was a pretty large island, it was 6940 feet across. They all loaded back up in the car and headed on around the lake. There were a lot of different pull offs, so you could view the lake. They would pull in to one overlook and then pull back out again.

Everyone was getting hungry so they decided to stop at a picnic area, which was called Cloud overlook. What a view, you could see for miles and miles and in the distance you could see another lake. This is the highest paved road in Oregon. The trees in that area are called Whitebark pine; they are dwarfed and contorted because of the harsh winds on top of the mountain in the winter.

They had their sandwiches and let the dogs run around for a little while and enjoyed the warm weather. It started to get a little windy but it was still fairly warm out, with just a touch of a chill in the air. They were glad that they had brought their light jackets with them.

After lunch they stopped at another overlook on the South rim. Another couple pulled in behind them. Aggie and her group were looking out toward the Pumice Castle. It is one of the most colorful features, which they had seen so far. It is a layer of orange pumice rock. According to the paper it has been eroded into the shape of a medieval castle.

Earl turned to see the other couples car rolling backward, heading toward the cliff. Earl first assumed that the couple was leaving, but as he turned around, there stood the couple. Earl yelled at them, "Your car is leaving, as he pointed at their car. The couple just stood there in shock, then the man ran toward the car, but it was too late.

The car was going over the edge, as everyone ran over to the edge of the cliff. The car headed down the crater wall, as if someone was driving it. All they could do is stand there in shock and wait for the car to hit the water. Then all of a sudden the car just stopped, right on the water's edge, as if someone had parked it down there.

They all just looked at each other; all they could do was laugh. Fred and Susan, the couple that just lost their car, just looked at each other. Fred just said, "What are we going to do now?" He wasn't really talking to anyone. Frank spoke up and told the couple they could give them a ride to the ranger office.

Susan and Fred said thanks, still in shock. It was a tight fit but everyone got into the truck. Aggie was sitting next to Susan, when it finally hit her; that their car went down a cliff. She asked Fred, "How in the hell are we going to get the car out of there. Fred just replied, "I'm just glad we took the dogs with us and we have car insurance." Aggie could tell Susan wanted to say something else, but she held her tongue, and just gave him a dirty look. Aggie figured Fred was the driver, he must not have put it in park, and Aggie could only assume that was what Susan was thinking too! They found the ranger station, and dropped Susan and Fred off, Fred thanked them, and disappeared into the station.

Wanda suggested, "Should we continue on with our trip? Hopefully, there won't be any more mishaps." Everyone laughed and agreed with her. Wanda being the tour guide said, "Next stop the Phantom Ship overlook! She began to read the information from the paper, "It was a formation of rocks that looked like a large sailing ship; the island is 16-stories high. It's made of eroded-resistant lave, 400,000 years old, it is the oldest exposed rock within the caldera."

As they turned into the overlook, they spotted a tour bus; Earl had to wonder who would take a tour bus here. From the sounds of the way they were talking, Frank said, "They were mostly Europeans." After everyone took pictures, and the ohh's and ahh's were done. They loaded up their bus and headed off. Frank said to Aggie, "I guess you're not the only one that wanted to see Crater Lake. They are coming all the way from Europe to see it!"

Wanda read from the brochure; "Next stop is Pinnacles Overlook. It consists of colorful spires, it is 100 feet tall, and it is being eroded away from the canyon wall. The Pinnacles are "Fossil Fumaroles" where volcanic gases rose up through a layer of volcanic ash, cementing the ash into solid rock." As they turned into the overlook, Aggie said, "This is beautiful, I would have never thought that those rocks were made out of ash."

They ended their visit at the Park Headquarters, where they saw the Vidae Falls. "It is a spring-fed creek which tumbled over a glacier-carved cliff and it dropped 100 feet over a series of ledges." Going to waterfalls is another thing that Frank and Aggie like to go see. Especially, since they have been traveling around Oregon. It was time to head back home; it was going to be a two hour ride back. Aggie turned to Wanda to thank her for being their tour guide today. Wanda replied, "Your welcome, and I do take tips!" Everyone laughed and Earl replied, "Put it on my tab!" All Wanda said was, "Yea Right!"

It was a nice drive back; it was just getting dark when they arrived home. Earl and Wanda headed home and Frank and Aggie took the girls for a walk. Frank and Aggie settled in for the night, Frank went to the bedroom to watch some TV and Aggie wanted to do some reading. She popped some popcorn, and sat down on the couch to read her book. She had closed the curtain earlier, something they did every night.

As she was sitting there she kept hearing noises. Then she heard something scratching on the window in the RV, right next to where she was sitting. Then it felt like the wind was rocking the RV. There was no wind that night and she knew Frank was in the bedroom. She couldn't figure out what it was, so she opened the curtains and there it was! There was a big nose of a bear on the window, sniffing and pawing at the window. It must have smelled the popcorn and was trying to figure out how to get it. The bear and Aggie just looked at each other, and then Aggie screamed called for Frank, "Frank, we have a problem, there is a bear at our window!!" As she backed away from the window. The bear was surprised to see a human, but didn't stop looking into the window. It still wanted the popcorn!

Frank came running out of the bedroom, asking "What did you say?" All Agatha could do is point at the window. Frank turned toward the window that Aggie was pointing at. There it was, a big black bear, looking into the window with his big claws scratching on it, and pushing on the window. They weren't too sure of what to do. They figured yelling at it, might scare it away or get it mad. But, maybe it would run away!

They started waving their arms and yelling, but it didn't move, it looked at them like they were crazy. They moved towards the window, and continued to wave and scream at the bear. The bear took off running, but then stopped and looked at them. Aggie wondered if he was thinking about coming back. But he didn't, he just walked off into the night.

The dogs weren't sure what was going on but they joined in the yelling by barking like crazy. The funny part was they were barking at Agatha and Frank, not the bear. Agatha turned to Frank and said, "No more popcorn for us!" They were just glad that they hadn't been out side with the dogs, when the bear decided to come around. It took a little while but they finally settled in for the night.

The next morning they started packing everything away that was set up outside. They were going to leave for Burns the next day, and just wanted to get a jump start. By the afternoon they had packed everything up outside of the rig, and rolled up the awning.

They wanted to check out a few more areas before leaving. They headed up to Newberry National Volcanic Monument. As they climbed up the mountain the weather started to get cold and wet, but that wouldn't stop them. Their first stop was the biggest lava flow in the world; it was a mountain of obsidian. It had stairs going up to the top, and once they got to the top, they could see for miles around. The obsidian was everywhere, all types of it.

As the day wore on the weather continued to get worse. It was starting to rain harder and the wind was picking up, it was time to go back down the mountain. Aggie didn't do well in cold weather. But they couldn't pass up the Paulina Falls; it was on the way down the mountain anyway. They hiked over to the falls; it wasn't too far from the parking lot and the weather was warmer lower on the mountain, but it was still raining a little bit.

The waterfalls were beautiful; there were two of them, right next to each other. The trees around the area were small pines. Some had weird shapes, and protrusions from their trunks. Of course, Frank had to point out one of the protrusions looked like breasts and another looked like a butt.

According to the sign by the waterfall, "The Paulina waterfall was 200 feet farther downstream, over 2000 years ago. It's not very far except moving those tons and tons of solid rock probably took just a few hours when it happened. During the flood the water flows rocketed to 10,000 ft. per second, it had moved the waterfall back 200 feet. That is 500 times more water and enough power to erode solid rock, snap trees off at roots and toss elephant-sized boulders miles down the stream."

As Frank and Agatha watched the waterfalls they could see where the water was coming from and it was a small creek. It was hard to believe that all that water was coming from that little creek. The wonders of Mother Nature! As they wandered back to the car they were surprised how many of the trees had unusual formations on their trunks. Again Mother Nature does the most unusual things and has a sense of humor! It was time to head home and get ready for the trip to Burns tomorrow.

CHAPTER 7

Burns, OR and then
to Nampa, ID

Agatha was getting a little antsy; she wanted to get on the road, and see another state. She also wanted to get some rock hounding done. She figured she must have gotten it from her mother. When her mother found a rock she liked she would have Agatha's dad load it up and take it home with them. Each time her parents moved from one house to another, they had to take all the rocks they had collected through the years, with them.

Aggie took it to the next level and she not only picked up rocks, she collected them from the Mineral and Rock shows they would go to. They also stopped at the rock store in the different states they went through. They also enjoyed going rock hounding. They knew that Burns, Oregon had a variety of obsidian and other stones in that area. Agatha had bought a book called "Western Gem Hunters Atlas," by Cy Johnson and son. This is how they started their rock hounding years ago.

It should only take three hours to get to Burns; they were going to set up camp at Burns RV campground for a couple of days and then go to Nampa, ID where Aggies's niece Ann and her family had just moved to. The last time she saw her was when they had returned from the Rosland Island. It was quite the family reunion; Aggie couldn't believe how many times people said, "We were sure you guys were dead. How was it living on an Island?" Aggie told Frank, "It will be great to see them, without the rest of the family around."

As Frank and Aggie left Bend, they headed toward Burns on Hwy 20. It started out with a few farms and then after awhile there wasn't anything to be seen except bushes and the high desert. It reminded them both of the deserts in Texas. After awhile there were rolling hills, and long straight highway for miles. Frank was in the lead this time, when he drives he keeps his eyes only on the road. He kept thinking to himself how small the road seamed. Every time a large truck would go by, he would hold his breath, it felt like there wasn't much room between them. On the other hand, Aggie could only see the back of the RV, so she would look around and enjoy the view.

The first seventy miles were pretty boring; the landscape was the same old thing, high desert and rolling hills. As they started climbing the mountain range, there were a few view points, where you could pull off and take in the view. It was beautiful from on top of the mountain, you could see into the different valleys, and the rolling hills below. There wasn't much out there, just land and the Snake River going through the valley. They went up and down mountains for the next sixty miles. In between the mountains they would follow the river for a little while, and then they would head up another mountain.

Frank and Aggie stopped in a little area along the side of the road. They wanted to let the dogs out and have a little break before stopping in Burns. The side of the road had old cottonwood trees; they were at least three feet across. It was in the 80's outside; needless to say it was nice to have the shade from the old trees. The dogs did their running around and were happy to get out of the RV, while Frank and Aggie had a little snack. They only had sixty miles to go, it was time to move on; it was a nice break for everyone.

They continued on Hwy 20, there are a lot more hills and long straight stretches to go. As they started coming off the last mountain range, they started seeing cattle and farm land. Aggie saw a herd of cattle on one side of the road, but as she got closer she noticed the cattle all had white butts. Then she saw it wasn't cattle, but white tail deer, there had to be fifty of them. She radioed Frank and asked him, "Do you see the deer?" He replied back, "No!" She told him to look to his right. Frank replied back, "Cool, thanks for telling me." Frank told Aggie later, that he would of never saw them if she wouldn't have radioed him.

They continued on, Aggie was about fifty feet behind Frank, when a coyote jump off the hill, which was on the side of the road. It looked like it was flying. It landed in between Frank and Angie rigs, it landed in the middle of the road, in a single bound and then to the other side. It all happened in the matter of seconds. The coyote disappeared into the desert. Aggie radioed Frank and told him what had just happened, all he said was "At least you didn't hit it."

After being on the road for three hours they arrived in Burns. It's a small country town. The RV campground was on the outskirts of town. It was a Good Sam; it was very clean and well kept. Frank and Aggie were planning on staying in Burns for a couple of days. They only set up what they needed, water, electric and sewage.

It had been a while since they had gone out for dinner, so they found a nice steak house in town. It turned out that it wasn't all that great and it was a little over priced. But Aggie figured at least she didn't have to cook or clean up after dinner. Sheba and Suzie were really good about staying in the RV by their selves, "Thank goodness, all they ever wanted was to go for a walk.

The next morning they got up early, normally they did every morning. But they wanted to go rock hounding before it got to hot. They loaded up their rock hounding equipment; hammer, bags, and water. The girls get to go with them this time. There was a rock store in town, they stopped by there first, to see what type of rocks or mineral that was in the area. They had gotten some maps from the lady at the RV camp, which showed where to look for stones. They had a good idea what area they should look in.

The rock store was run by an older gentleman, and the store filled with all types of stones. Aggie couldn't help but think about her collection and how it would put this store to shame. The owner of the store wasn't much of a talker though, so they didn't get much information from him.

The map they had received from the lady at the campground was a little off, but they finally found the road that they needed to be on. It was five miles closer to their camp, than the map had shown. After a morning of walking around in the desert, they found what they were looking for, different types of obsidian. They found a lot of small piece of obsidian, called Apache tears. It is obsidian that you can see light through. There is a lot of Sheen rock in the area too; it is another type of volcanic rock. It was starting to get hot outside, and the dogs were finally getting tired. It was time to go back to the campground.

After sitting around the campground for a little while, Frank and Aggie decided to go explore the town. It wasn't that far away so they walked to it. As they walked around the neighborhoods, they started spotting old cars, parked in people yards. In other yards there was junk piled high. Some of the houses looked to be pretty old. But in the middle of this neighborhood, was a really nice park. It had a big play ground, with picnic tables and even a restroom. It was funny because right across the street there was an old Hamm's beer building. The building had to be built in early 1900.

Frank and Aggie continued to walk around the town, there weren't any dates on the buildings. Frank and Aggie had tried to go to the museum, but it was closed. They both enjoyed checking out town's museum, it made the town come alive with history. Otherwise, it's just an old town, in need of repairs.

It was getting late, it was time to walk back to the RV, and get ready to head to Nampa, ID. It was only 175 miles away, on Hwy 20; it should only take three to four hours.

The first two hours were uneventful; it was pretty much the same as the first part of Hwy 20. But as they got closer to Nampa, they went over bigger mountains. Frank was still in front, as Aggie followed behind, when all of a sudden Frank hit his brakes. There was a herd of antelopes in the middle of the road. He radio back to Aggie, and told her, "There is a herd of white tail antelope standing in the middle of the road." Aggie could see them walking in front of the RV, from behind the rig.

Frank honked at them, and they just looked at him. Then the car from the other direction started honking. Still the antelope just stood there. The driver on the other side got out of his car and started waving his arms and yelling. There were a couple of bucks that didn't like it, so they started to go after the guy. He ran to his car and the bucks were right behind him. He jumped into his car and just had enough time to close the door. Both of the bucks started attacking the car. It didn't take long before the bucks got bored and moved on. After that no one wanted to get out of their cars, because they didn't know what the antelope would do.

Finally after honking for awhile, the antelope started to wonder off to the other side of the road. There had to be seventy of them, and they were not in a hurry to get out of the way. After about twenty minutes they started to move off the road, Frank and Aggie continued on their way.

After four hours they made it to the Freeway 84, and then into Idaho. There was a visitor center just inside the Idaho border; it was also a rest area. They stopped there to get information about Idaho, and take the girls for a walk. They only had another thirty miles to go to Ann's place. Frank and Aggie were getting into their rigs, when Aggie called to Frank, "Only thirty miles to go!" Frank called back, "Yea, for now, but the good news is we are finally out of Oregon!"

CHAPTER 8

Nampa, ID

It didn't take long to get to Ann and Howard's house. Ann and the kids must have seen them pull in. Before they even stopped the rigs, they were all out there to greet them. It was great to see them, there were hugs all around.

Frank wanted to get Penelope set up before doing anything else. It is a military thing, according to Aggie. Once everything was set up, they got a tour of Ann and Howard's new home. They lived on the outskirts of Nampa, Idaho. Their house was out in the country. It has three floors, a large yard, a little cabin outback and to top it off a swimming pool. It was huge, needless to say, the house and yard was beautiful!

They parked Penelope next to the house in the driveway. The nice thing about where they were located allowed Agatha and Frank to take their walks in the evening. Ann and Howard lived on a country road, which was a half mile loop and close to Lake Lowell; it was a man-made lake built in 1905 and was completed by 1910. It was set up as a wildlife reserve. There were thousands of birds throughout the reservation.

The first couple of days, Frank and Aggie hung out around the house. After being on the road, Frank and Aggie had gained some weigh so they decided to walk every day, their goal is to walk five miles a day. So far they have only done it four times, in the last six weeks. The nice thing was the lake was only a half mile away.

On their first walk at Lowell Lake, they climbed up the 150 stairs to get to the top of the dam, and then walked along the dam rim. The area around the dam was a wildlife reserve. There were hundreds of birds, not only in the water but in the trees. They discovered later that there were just as many bugs in the air as there were birds, if not more. In the field they were walking through at the bottom of the dam, there were all types of flying bugs. You would think with all these birds around there would be less bugs!

Frank and Aggie continued to walk every day, each time in a different direction or area of the park. Ann also enjoyed walking with them, when she had the time. Ann and Howard both went for a walk with Frank and Aggie; they ended up walking along new trails. The area they were walking in was an open field area, which was part of the reserve. As they were walking, they realize they had forgotten their water; it was in the 80s, so they didn't want to be out in the heat for too long. After an hour they headed over to the visitor center, there was a sign saying the trail was closed. They all just laughed and decided to walk back to the car on the road, instead of taking the hiking trail back. Howard said, "I guess they forgot to put a sign at the other end. Frank wondered how they could close an open area from the public.

The next week was nice, they enjoyed the weather, and it was in the 70s most of the time. The only complaint was that the flies were everywhere, each time they would open their RV door the flies would fly in by the dozens. Another problem was Suzie hated the fly swatter. Every time they used the fly swatter Suzie would start barking and jumping at it. It became a game; they would take Suzie outside, and start killing the flies. Suzie would hear the swatting, and would come running back into the RV. Aggie would hide the swatter behind her back, while Susie would run around trying to find it.

Most of the walks went without any issues, but there were a couple of things that made the walks more interesting. One time while they were walking over by the dam, they ran into a three foot snake. It was just lying in the middle of the path, it was very still. Frank touched it with his walking stick, and it moved just a little bit and the tongue started flicking in and out. It looked like it had just eaten something; it had a four inch lump in the middle of his long body. They decided to give the snake its space, as they moved away the snake just laid there, enjoying the evening and its dinner.

On another walk, Frank and Aggie were walking the girls, Aggie had Susie and Frank had Sheba. Aggie and Frank noticed a, medium white dog at the next door neighbors. It was trying to jump the fence and was barking at them as they walked by. With each leap the white dog came closer and closer to clearing the fence.

Aggie started pulling Susie back to her, and then it happened. Frank had already picked up Sheba, when the white dog cleared the fence. It came running as fast as it could down the drive way toward them. Aggie pulled Susie to her just in time, as she lifted Susie up the white dog hit Aggies's arm and hand. Susie yelped as Aggie put her on her shoulder. Aggie wasn't sure if the dog had gotten a hold of Susie or Susie just yelps because she was scared.

Frank was behind Aggie, and saw the dog coming to attack; he already had Sheba in his arms. He handed Sheba to Aggie and tried to protect them. Frank came at the white dog and knocked the dog off Aggie. Frank hit the dog with his fist and then kicked the dog, as he was coming back for another attack. As Frank went to kick the dog again, he lost his balance and fell to the ground. Well it was more of a spin, and then it looked like he just sat down.

The white dog, started to run away, then it looked like he changed his mind and was coming back, when the owner yelled at him to "Come here!" It must have been quite a site, Aggie standing there with both the dogs on her shoulder, bleeding from her hand and Frank sitting on the ground trying to protect them.

The owner put the dog into their backyard and came to see if Frank and Aggie were ok. Aggie told the owner, she was ok and showed her the cut and bite mark on her hand. Susie and Sheba weren't too sure what had just happened, but they had no problem staying in Aggie arms. Frank was up on his feet in seconds, and wasn't a happy camper. The owner apologized over and over, and to let her know if they needed anything. Aggie was starting to feel the pain from the cuts. She was just glad, she didn't get bitten by the dog, it was just a claw marks across the back of her right hand and it looked like a little bite on the other hand.

It all happen so fast, one minute the white dog is jumping up and down trying to jump the fence, which was a good twenty-five feet away. The next minute it was all over with, they had been attacked and were walking back to Ann's house.

The owner was Ann's next door neighbor, so they didn't have far to walk back. As Frank and Aggie were walking back to the house, Frank said, "The one time we don't take our walking stick, we get attacked!" They both smiled at each other, and agreed "Never again!

Aggie and Frank went into Ann's house to wash out the cut, of course Aggie had to show Ann her battle wound. Ann went into mother mode and started asking all kinds of questions. Did the dog have it shots? Where is the dog now? Aggie agreed they should go ask the neighbor about the shots. Good news the dog had its shots. Well another day in the world of Frank and Aggie!

The next couple of days went without any events; they decided to go to the lake to walk their dogs and to get their excise. Then the storm front came in, it started blowing and raining for the next couple of days. It was time to move on. Ann and Howard wanted to go camping with Frank and Aggie, they agreed on going to Twin Falls, ID for the weekend. Frank and Aggie would head out in the morning and Ann and Howard would join them later in the afternoon.

There really isn't much to see between Nampa and Twin Falls, it pretty much looks the same, rolling hills and lots of high desert. Frank and Aggie arrived at the campground around noon and set up camp. A couple of hours later Ann and family showed up. It was nice; they parked next to each other with their doors facing each other. The play ground was next to them, so the kids had a great time.

The next morning everyone loaded up into the van and headed into town. They went to the visitor center to check out what was around there. To get to the center, they had to cross the Snake River; it had a large bridge called Perrine Memorial Bridge. In the valley below, there were golf courses and you could see the geological history of the area on the canyon walls. The different colors on the canyon walls were beautiful when the sun hit them.

What they really came to see were the waterfalls, the Twin Falls and the Shoshone falls. Aggie was talking to the visitor center host, and the host told her that both of the waterfalls had been turned off. She explained that they had to do maintenance on the dams, so the falls would be closed until March. Aggie told Ann and Howard the news, "The waterfalls are closed due to maintenances." Aggie smiled at them. They didn't believe her at first, but she assured them that it was true.

It is hard to believe that humans can just turn off a waterfall these days, but they can. They all agreed to walk around the canyon wall and watch the Parching jumpers, jump off the bridge. If you were just looking at the bridge, and watching a person climbing over the bridge wall, you would never know that they had parachutes. Mostly because you couldn't see it, it was in their back pack.

As Aggie and her group watch the jumpers, climb over the bridge wall, and stand on the lip on the other side of the wall of the bridge, and then jump into the canyon below. They would jump out as far as they could and then release their parachute, and floating down to the bottom of the canyon. Of course they had to be careful not to land in the Snake River below. There were five different jumpers; it was fun to watch them. The only problem Aggie could see in doing this was that they had to climb back up the hill, which wasn't an easy climb. But Aggie figured if that was what they enjoyed doing, more power to them! She may have tried it when she was in her twenties, but she wouldn't do it now. Frank was in the same frame of mind as Aggie, it looked like fun otherwise.

Next stop was the Twin Falls and the Shoshone waterfalls; they stopped by the visitor center and purchased post cards of the waterfall, when they had water coming down them. This way they could see the difference before and after. It was amazing to look at the post cards and then look at where the falls were suppose to be. All that was there now was a small waterfall with a little bit of water coming down off the wall, and a few pools of water. The rocks were grey and smooth. Where the water could reach there was green algae on the rocks. There were doves and other birds living on the walls across from the falls. At the bottom of the falls the water was a dark green but as the water moved down the canyon the water turned a beautiful dark blue.

Frank said, "I'm sure, not too many people have seen it like this before!" Aggie agreed it was interesting to see what the water was hiding; there was even a road at the bottom of the falls. You can't see it when the water is running, but with the water turned off, it was easy to see.

After looking at both falls, they found a nice park to stop at. It was next to a lake, this was a great place for the kids to let off some steam. It was fun to watch the kids; they were having so much fun. They have so much energy; even Howard was climbing and enjoying the park. It reminded them of their grandkids in Texas.

For lunch that day they found a hamburger place to eat at and then they headed to the toy store that Howard had spotted earlier in the day. The store had toys for all ages and fudge of all favors. Frank and Aggie tasted most of the fudge before leaving the store. It was hard for Aggie to leave the store without any fudge, it was soooo good. But they did, and headed back to camp.

Where they had a started a campfire and made smores. Ann had made little bags with everything you need to make smores with. Then it was movie time, it was close to

Halloween. They had to watch Halloween Town; it was something Ann's family did every year.

The next morning Frank and Aggie were bound for Las Vegas and Ann and Howard would be heading home. Aggie got up early to do some laundry before they headed out to Ely, NV.

Everyone else was still in bed; she carried the laundry basket over to the building where the facility was located. She started loading the clothes into the washers, when she noticed a pile of clothes in the corner. She thought it was rather strange, and curiosity got the better of her. As she walked over to the pile of clothes, it started moving. It made her nervous; she thought maybe there was a rat inside or some other kind of animal. Then she realized that either it was a huge rat or there was a person underneath the clothes.

She nudged on the pile of clothes and said, "Hello is someone in there? To Aggies surprise a young girl head slowly came out of the pile of clothes. She looked scared half to death, her hair was a mess. Aggie assured her that it was okay and she wouldn't harm her. Aggie helped her get off of the floor and had her sit in the chair and then asked her, "What is your name? What are you doing here?"

Aggie could tell that she still wasn't too sure of her. She tried to reassure her again, that she wasn't going to hurt her or tell on her that she was there. The girl finally told Aggie that she had ran away from home and was headed to Las Vegas. Her family lived in Baker City, OR and she just couldn't stand living in a small town anymore. She said, "She wanted to go somewhere where there was excitement. She had been on the road for a couple weeks, the she has been hitchhiking. She and a friend had started out together, but her friend had taken off with a guy they had met at a rest area. So she was all alone, but was determined to get to Las Vegas. But now she wasn't so sure. She didn't want to tell Aggie her name, but Aggie convinced her to at least tell her, her first name. She finally told Aggie her name, it was Darlene. But she refused to tell Aggie her last name.

Aggie told Darlene why don't you come over to our RV and get something to eat and get warmed up. If you want me to, I will give you some shampoo and soap so you can take a shower afterwards. Darlene agreed to go with her back to the RV. Aggie finished loading up the washer machine and they both headed back to camp.

Frank was sitting on the couch drinking coffee, and watching the news when Aggie came in and told him we have a visitor. Frank assumed that it was Ann or one of the kids. But to his surprise it was a total stranger, and to top it off, it was a teenage girl and by all appearances she looked homeless.

Aggie introduced Darlene to Frank and explained that she was a runaway and she found her in the laundry room earlier. Frank asked Darlene to take a seat and asked if she would like a cup of coffee or maybe some hot chocolate. Darlene said, "Hot chocolate! That would be great. Frank got up and went to the kitchen and started making hot chocolate for Darlene. Frank wasn't sure why Aggie brought a homeless girl into their RV, but he knew to just go along with her.

Aggie offered her some cereal for breakfast and slowly but surely got information from her about where her parents lived. Darlene started talking about being on the road and all the weirdoes that were out there. After about an hour, Aggie had found out Darlene's parents names and phone number. Darlene was ready to go home, now the problem was to figure out how to get her home. Aggie suggested to Darlene that she go take a shower and get cleaned up. When she got back, they would give her parents a call and figure out how they could get her home.

While Darlene was in the shower, Ann and Howard came out of their trailer. Aggie explained to them about Darlene and how she had discovered her in the laundry room and what was going on. They were all sitting at the picnic table when Darlene came back from the showers. She looked like a totally different girl all cleaned up. Darlene acted a little nervous as she got closer to the picnic table; Aggie got up and lightly touched her on the arm and introduced her to Ann and Howard. At first Darlene was a little shy but after she sat down and started talking to Ann and Howard and found out that they had teenage daughters she felt like she could talk to them.

She explained why she ran away from home, she told them how boring it was in their little town, and how boring her parents' were. But after being on the road, she learned that boredom isn't such a bad thing after all.

Aggie suggested that she call her parents and let them know that she is safe and wanting to come home, Darlene agreed. Darlene walked away from the group, so she could have some privacy. Ann and Howard had already agreed to take Darlene back with them to Nampa, Idaho and her parents can pick her up from there. Darlene's parents asked to talk to Aggie and Ann; they thanked them for helping their daughter. They told them that they have been looking everywhere for her. Darlene's parents were happy that Ann could bring Darlene back as far as Nampa.

Ann gave Darlene's parents their address and told them they should be home around four. Darlene parent's told Ann they will be there as soon as they could. Ann handed the phone back to Darlene; Darlene started crying and was telling her folks how much she loved them. Aggie and Ann both had tears in their eyes. It was then that, Aggie remembered that she still had laundry to do; she headed back to the laundry room.

She left Darlene with Ann and her family, Darlene seemed to be doing ok with them. Darlene stayed in Aggie and Frank's RV that night, it didn't take Darlene long to fall asleep. Aggie figured this was the first time, in a long time that Darlene felt safe. The next morning Aggie made a big breakfast for the three of them, and then took Darlene over to Ann's trailer.

It was time for Frank and Aggie to move forward on their adventures. The plan was to stop in Ely, NV and then stop in Alamo, NV; they would only spend one night at each campground. Normally, they could make the trip in six hours, but they wanted to take their time. The half way mark to Vegas would be Ely, NV.

As they left Twin Falls, ID they headed toward Jackpot, NV, they stopped for a break there and let the girls out for a little bit. They got back on to Hwy 93, next stop Wells, NV. As they were going down Hwy 93 Aggie noticed there were high chain link fencing running along both sides of the road. Which was weird, normally it is just barb wire fencing. As they continued down the road, there was an overpass going over the Hwy, but no roads or reason to have them there. No town or farmer as far as she could tell. It just didn't make since to her, then she remembered seeing signs before the fencing which said, "Watch out for animals!"

This was "Open range," the fencing was to keep the animals off the road. The over passes were to let the animals cross in safety. As they were getting closer to Wells, the fencing disappeared. Aggie thought to herself, she never did see any animals of any type, no cattle or deer. They stopped in Wells to get gas; she had to know if she was right about the fencing. She asked the clerk at the gas station and she confirmed what Aggie had guessed. The clerk said, "It was to save the animals, but also the accident rate involving animals decreased by 90%." Aggie had to wonder how many people drove down that road, and never realize there was a fence and over passes for just the animals. She couldn't help but tell Frank about it and what a great idea it was.

The landscape was pretty much the same as the rest of the trip, high desert; it was one valley after another. They would go for miles, up and down hills and then come back down into another valley. Some of the valley names were: Pub Valley, Clover Valley, Bluff Valley, and Dry Lake Valley this was just a few of the names.

They arrived in Ely around four and started looking for a campground; they found one on the other side of town. Frank liked driving threw the town and finding a place to camp on the same side they would be leaving from in the morning. That way he doesn't have to deal with the morning traffic, even in a small town it can be a pain.

The campground was a KOA, it was really nice, and everyone was very friendly. The campground had old cover wagons sitting around, they were all fixed up. It is interesting how friendly people are in campgrounds. Aggie just couldn't get over the difference in how sociable people are or were when they are camping.

Aggie as usual wanted to check into the history of Ely, even if they couldn't check out the town. The brochure she found had some interesting information about Ely, "Ely was founded as a stagecoach station along the Pony Express and Central Overland Route. Ely's mining boom came later than the other towns around it. So with the discovery of copper in 1906, Ely became a mining town. It suffered through the boom-and-bust cycles that were common in the West at that time. Ely was home to a number of copper mining companies, Kennecott being the most famous.

There was a crash in the copper market in the mid-1970s, Kennecott shut down and copper mining disappeared. The town was first called Ely in 1878 in honor of Smith Ely, president of the Selby Copper Mining and Smelting Company.

Ely has a tourism center, and is home of the Nevada Northern Railway Museum, which has the Ghost Train of Old Ely, a working steam-engine passenger train that travels the historic tracks from Ely to the Robinson mining district. There is also the historic six-story Hotel Nevada located in downtown Ely. The hotel opened in 1929, and it was the tallest building in Nevada well into the 1940s and was the state's first fire-proof building."

Aggie called Ann that evening to see how everything went with Darlene. Ann told her, "Darlene was getting a little nervous, but Ann could tell she was also excited to go home."

The next stop would be Alamo, NV, when driving a RV; it can add a lot of time to any trip, hopefully it will only take about four hours. They settled in for the night. They planned on leaving around 10, that should put them into Alamo around two o'clock.

Frank and Aggie arrived in Alamo, and drove right threw it. Frank pulled off to the side of the road with the RV, and Aggie pulled in behind him. Frank radioed Aggie and asked her to go find the campground they were going to stay at for the night. Aggie agreed and drove down the road to make sure there wasn't another city over the hill. There wasn't, they had seen signs that said the city they just drove through was Alamo. All they could see of it from the road was a single truck stop. Aggie back tracked to the town hidden behind a tree line and the truck stop, and sure enough it was Alamo.

She radioed Frank and told him to come on back, she was at the truck stop, and the campground they were looking for was behind the truck stop.

Once Frank arrived she took the lead and showed him the campground. It was a small place, but nice, it was run by an older lady and her son. Aggie went into the office, to pay for the night. The ladies son, George helped Frank back the RV, into their space. The campground was pretty empty, they arrived at two and by six, and the campground was full. This one was a Good Sam, it was clean and Frank and Aggie could walk to the truck stop. Later they drove around the town, it was a nice place.

There wasn't much information about the town, but Aggie did find this, "Alamo is about 90 miles from Las Vegas by way of Hwy 93. Its elevation is 3,449 feet (1,051 m). It was founded in 1901; Alamo is named after the Spanish word for "poplar" due to the localized presence of that type of tree." Aggie had guessed the trees that were around the campground were Poplar.

It was a nice evening, so they sat outside, and talked about their trip today. Aggie pointed out to Frank, that each valley they drove though had different plants. It was small cedar trees, and Joshua trees, and the next valley wouldn't have anything growing. Then it would start all over again. Except for the plants, there was nothing out there. It was mile after mile of high desert. Frank laughed and had to agree with her, the landscape didn't change much.

There wasn't much to do in the town, so they walked over to the truck stop and purchased some ice cream. The truck stop was also the grocery store for the town. Next stop Las Vegas, it should only take a couple hours, their plan was to stay in Vegas for three weeks, at the RV resort they had a membership at. They didn't unload anything at this stop;

Frank just connected the power up and called it good. The next morning they were ready to go by 9:00. Aggie told Frank, it will be nice to stay in a place where they will have septic connection. Frank had to agree, it is a pain to have to fill their "portable tank" and drag it off to a dump site.

The next 60 miles, were very uneventful. They saw one accident that involved a car carrier. Somehow or another the back car came loose and came out onto the road, which caused a fire. By the time that Frank and Agatha were driving by the fire department had already been working to put out the fire. The car that had fallen off of the rig, was just sitting on the side of the road. It looked like no one else was involved in the accident.

As they drove from one valley to the next Agatha noticed the difference in the desert landscape. She first thought there wasn't much difference between the valleys. But in the beginning of one valley there were small cedar trees and as they dropped in elevation, there were small Joshua trees, which grew bigger as they moved though the valleys. As they climbed over the next mountain and back down it would just be the opposite, it would be larger Joshua trees and then bigger cedar trees again. In one valley there was absolutely nothing except sagebrush, there wasn't even a bird in the sky.

Aggie was surprised how much landscape was the same from Nampa, Idaho all the way through to Las Vegas. She had found a shortcut on the paper map; the GPS always showed them the freeway route. They wanted to avoid the freeway as much as possible, when they were driving the RV. The new route not only avoided the freeway, but it also cut off 40 miles.

CHAPTER 9

Welcome to Las Vegas

Frank and Agatha finally made it to Las Vegas. Now the hard part was finding the RV campground they had made reservations at. After a few U-turns they decided to have Frank park the RV, while Aggie would go find the campground. So Frank parked the rig while Aggie drove around trying to find the campground. To her surprise it was only a block down the road. She called Frank on the two way radio and told him where to go. Within minutes Frank arrived at the new campground.

The campground was pretty much a parking lot; the spots were so close together, there was only room enough for a picnic table between them, if you were lucky! There really wasn't any room to put out their awning. But it did have all the important things: electricity, water and a septic outlet. The plan was to stay in Las Vegas for three weeks.

After they settled in they walked around the campground. It had cinderblock wall for the fence with barbwire on top of that; Aggie figured it was to keep people out. Frank pointed out to Aggie that it felt like a prison, more than a RV campground. This was a far cry from the last few places they had stayed at. The other places that they stayed, had trees and plenty of space to themselves. Frank said, "Are we sure we want to stay here for three weeks?" Aggie replied, well if it gets be too much, we can always leave!

In the next couple of days, they didn't do much, they went to a few casinos, and there were a couple of them in walking distance from the campground. After they walked to one of the casinos they understood why their RV campground had cinderblocks and barbwire around the campground, it wasn't the best of neighborhoods that's for sure.

Early one morning they went down to the strip to check out what was new down there. It was always amazing to see what they had done. They were surprised how many people was there that early in the morning, walking the strip. Aggie guessed they all had the same idea, because at night time you could barely get through anywhere. People are not as friendly as the campground people. They would run into you and not say excuse me or anything else. It was definitely a younger crowd than at the campground. Of course, they had to do a little bit of gambling, but after losing $40 in 15 minutes they decided that was enough of that.

Aggie and Frank both agreed that it was more fun and of more interesting to go see the sites around Las Vegas, and not only that it would be a lot cheaper than gambling. When they got home that afternoon Aggie pulled out her rock hounding book to see if there was anything good to go rock hounding for in the area. They found a place about 45 minutes away, which looked interesting; it even had a ghost town close to it.

The next day they packed a picnic basket and loaded the dogs up and headed out towards Beatty, NV. There were a couple of areas that looked promising for rock hounding. According to the book they should find some Rhyolite, Carrara Marble and Jasper.

There were a couple of small mining towns on the way to Beatty; there was Pahrump, Lathrop Wells and Indian Springs. There wasn't much to the towns, but at one time it looked like they were thriving places. There was an old fashion hotel, and another old building on Main Street, other than that there wasn't much.

The girls (dogs) started barking, which only meant they needed to take a potty break or get a drink. Either way we needed to stop somewhere offs the main road. Aggies's spotted a road that left the main road, so she drove down the road and headed up into the desert. As soon as the doors opened the dogs jumped out. Aggie thought to herself, I guess they really had to go.

As they checked out the area they discovered some interesting rocks and then of course there were places that people had dumped their junk. But in one of the piles of junk they found a large flat red rock, it was one of those decorative paving stone that people usually buy at the store. They smiled at each other and said why not? Aggie went down the road to bring up the Jeep; the rock was too heavy to carry it all the way down the hill. They loaded up the rock and the dogs and headed down the road.

As they came over the mountain they could see a little town in the distance. According to the map they had, there shouldn't have been a town in that valley. Of course, they had to go explore the town. But as they were driving towards the town, they spotted an abandoned gravel pit. There was no way that they were going to bypass that. You never know what type of rocks you will find in a gravel pit.

The gravel pit looked like it hadn't been used in a very long time. Suzie the adventurous one took off running into the field, she was checking out every little thing. Frank was calling to her to come back, that's when he heard a little rattle. He knew what it was immediately and stopped. He started backing out the way he had come in. He called to Aggie, "There are rattlesnakes out here! Frank started calling to Suzy, this time in his strong voice. Suzie knew when Frank used his strong voice she better get her butt back to him. They put the dogs inside of the Jeep, so they were safe. Suzy wasn't too happy about being left in the car.

But curiosity got the better of them. They both walked around the area where Frank had heard the rattlesnake. They were smart enough to come from the other direction. They also kept an ear open, just in case there were other rattlers around. They moved closer to where Frank had heard the first rattle, they slowed down. They were as quite as they could be, they could hear Suzie barking in the distance, she really didn't like being left in the car. Then they heard the rattle, Aggie was surprised that they had heard it, but sure enough there it was a rattlesnake. It was ready to strike; it was curled up and was on the alert. Frank figured it was at least 4 foot long, not a bad size for rattlesnake. The snake was watching them and it was ready to protect itself. Frank would move to one side and the snakes head would follow him, and then follow Frank back and forward. They didn't what to upset the snake anymore than they already had, so they backed up the same way they came in. They didn't want to get any closer to the snake.

Aggie asked Frank, What is the biggest rattlesnake you have seen? Frank said, "The biggest one he had seen in the wild was a seven foot long, if not longer. It was when he was out in the field at Fort Hood. He was setting up a site, when he looked down and he saw the snake, he almost stepped on it. The rattlesnake didn't care one way or another about him. The snake was crawling along with a big lump in its stomach. All it wanted to do is find a nice place to enjoy its meal. I just stood there and waited for it to disappear. Once it was gone, I finished my job and made sure I told my people to keep a watch out for it." As they were walking back to the car, he asked Aggie, "How about you?" Aggie said, "The only time I've seen a rattlesnake in the wild was in Eastern Oregon when we were driving around out there. But it was just a small little fella." The only other time that I've seen rattlesnakes up close is when we went to the rattlesnake round up in Texas. Aggie recalled the time that we had went to the round up with their friends.

It was when the kids were younger, and they had heard about the Rattlesnake round up. None of us had ever seen one, so we loaded up the kids and headed towards Sweethome, TX. They have been doing this since 1958; it's on the second weekend of March. It was in Nolan County Coliseum, we had to park in a newly mowed hay field. Aggie asked Frank, remember how crowded it was, who would ever thought that so many people wanted to see rattlesnakes. Anyway, we were in line waiting when the girls, started getting scared about seeing all those snakes. After awhile we gave in and headed back to our cars.

As we round the corner of the building we could see smoke, coming from the direction of our cars. It didn't take us long to connect the dotted lines. Ricky yelled "Our cars!" The guys ran over to the cars that were parked side by side. There was a row of cars parked on both sides of the row they were in. The rest of us weren't far behind; all we could do is stand back and watch.

We could see the fire was surrounding the cars. There were people trying to put out the fire, but to no avail. The guys jumped though the fire and got into their vehicles. Frank and Aggies truck started right up and Frank drove the truck out of the fire. But Ricky's car didn't start; the flames were coming up under the rear of Rick's car. The tail lights were even beginning to melt as he got into his car. By this time Frank had already moved their truck to a safe place and could not understand what the problem was with Ricky. Why he was taking so long to move. They all started yelling for him to get out, but he was determined to save their car.

Just as the flames started to move under his car, Ricky jumped out of the car. They thought he was going to abandon it, and then he got back into the car. Started it up and pulled away from the fire, the space under his car caught fire, and was completely in flames in seconds. Then the fire trucks came pulling into the field, and within minutes the fire was out. Needless to say, we were all very happy to see the cars were all safe. Luckily their truck was unharmed, and Ricky's car ran and could be driven. But Ricky's car did have some scorched paint and burned tail light lenses and wiring. It could have been much worse.

Frank asked Ricky, "Why didn't you get out of there?" Ricky told him, he was so nervous his knees were shaking and he could not let out the clutch. It was then that Ricky could hear a hissing noise coming from his gas cap. He thought it might blow if he didn't release the pressure. That's why he jumped out of the car and took off the gas cap. Then jumped back into the car, and this time he knew he had to go or blow up and he did pull out without a second to spare.

We found out later that it was the Cadillac's cataleptic converter, which was sitting next to Ricky's car. The Cadillac didn't do so well, its tires had caught fire and the underside was all burned up. Ricky's car had the back side all burned, and a lot of the wiring was shot. But they drove it back to their house; we followed behind them because their lights didn't work anymore. It was a good thing the girls didn't want to see the snakes. The only snakes we saw that day were the ones in the boxes by the entrances way. Frank laughed and said, "Yea, that was exciting, I'm just glad the truck started up!"

By this time, they were in the town they had seen from the mountain, it was strange. As they drove down one street, which they assumed was Main Street, all the roads to the left were closed to cars. There were houses on the roads, and large buildings by each of the houses. Frank asked Aggie, doesn't this look like runways, and she agreed. But there weren't any airplanes in site. As they continued along the main road they spotted a sign that said, "Air City." Now it all made since, the people that live here, fly in and the large buildings were their garage for their airplane. They finally found a road they could turn on, they just drove around the area, when they found a small business area. There wasn't much there, a post office, pizza place and a tavern. It was time to head back to camp, two hours later they were back at camp, outside of Las Vegas.

The dogs were ready to settle in for the night. But they needed to go for a walk, before calling it a night; it would be a short walk. When Sheba doesn't what to walk, she'll just sit down or she will turn around and head back home. Somehow she always knows which direction to go. They have now been in Vegas for a week, two more weeks to go. Tomorrow they are going to visit St. George, UT. Aggie had once thought of going to college there, but instead she joined the army. Frank was interested in the history in that area.

Aggie, just for fun had started writing down the names of the different rigs they have seen; drive past their campsite and in the campground. After a week, the list was getting to long. Here's the list for one week:

Arctic fox	Imperial	Flair	Holiday Rambler
Voyage	Dutch star	Cheetah	Raptor
Polar mist	Sunnybrook	Springdale	Flagstaff
Passport	Pioneer	Nash	Springdale
Track	Cameo	Endeavor	Midas
Alpenlite	Knight	Seaview	Wilderness advantage
Allison bus	Wildwood	Amazon Lite	Americana
Outback	Terry	Southwind	Mountain View
Big Sky	Atrium	Avalanche	Rampage
Vacationer	Expedition	Trek	Sundance
Open range	Teton home	Meridian	Flagstaff
North country	Everest	Wildwood	Seahawk
Bullet	Freedom Express	Double diplomat	Alpha
Bouncer	Forest River	Airbus	Glacier Peak
Cambria	Tuscany	Raptor	Cougar
Voltage	Pinnacle	Discover America	Dolphin
Cameo	Dutch star	Country coach	Coachman
Night	Airstream	Hitchhiker	Denali
Sunnybrook	Denali	Neptune	Prowler
Seahawk	Road Warrior	Montana fifth wheel	Big country
Passport	Silverback	Cooper Canyon	Solitude
High Country Montana	Wilderness trailer	Patriot thunder	Ciara
Holiday Rambler	Eagle	Pace arrow	Scamper
Ambassador	Itasca		

After a week Aggie gave up. Her conclusion was there are a lot of different types of RVs.

The next morning they were off to St. George, UT, it was only 125 miles away. The trip didn't take too long; their first stop was at the Wild Life Museum at the Dixie Center. It was amazing, it was huge, and according to the flyer the facility was over 35,000-square-foot. It had more than 300 species of wildlife created; they used fiberglass or foam forms and real skin and fur to create them.

The animals were displayed in their native habitat—which included Africa, the Arctic, Asia, Australia, Europe, and North America. The two waterfalls cascade from the second floor down to the first floor, there are hidden speakers that provided ambient wildlife and nature sounds.

As Frank and Aggie walked around, they couldn't believe how real all the animals looked. Each area had a sign with a number, so you could enter that number on the hand held device and hear more information about each of the animals. There are so many different animals, but the ones that caught their attention the most were the Saiga Antelope. "The Saiga is recognizable by an extremely unusual, over-sized, flexible nose structure, the proboscis.

During summer migrations the Saigas' nose helps filter out dust kicked up by the herd and cools the animal's blood. In the winter it heats up the frigid air before it is taken to the lungs." The other one is the Chinese Water Deer. "The water deer have developed long canine teeth which protrude from the upper jaw (tusks) like the canines of musk deer. The canines are fairly large in the bucks, ranging in length from 5.5 cm / 2.1 in. on average to as long as 8 cm / 3.2 in. Does, the female of the breed, in comparison have tiny canines, which are on average 0.2 in. in length."

In some of the displays animals were attacking other animals. As Frank and Aggie continued to walk around the museum, they listened to the hand held radio; they were given at the beginning. The radio would tell them about the different animals that were on display. Aggie found it interesting how many rich people would take animals that were going extinct, and protect them by having them moved to their private property. They would raise them until the herd would grow strong in numbers. Some would go back to their original area and others would stay on the land they grew up on.

After lunch they drove to Leed, UT, where there was a Civilian Conservation Corp camp, (CCC), during the depression era. This was a program to provide much needed employment starting in 1933. They are in the progress of preserving and restoring the area. It was built on a hill; it was hard to believe that so many people lived there, over a hundred men.

As they walked the trails, they came down the hill and spotted an old cottonwood tree. It was hollow inside, and the trunk was split wide open. and yet it was still alive. Aggie had Frank go on the other side of the tree and photographed him looking through the hole. This area wasn't much different than where Aggie was raised, in Delta City, UT.

The weather forecast had reported there was going to be a cold front coming in with strong winds. Frank wanted to be home before the 50 miles an hour wind came in. Suddenly it started to get cold and breezy, it was time to head back to Vegas. On the way back to Vegas the wind started picking up. There was nothing out there to stop the wind, there was nothing but desert as far as you could see, and as flat as a pancake. The road from St. George to Vegas crossed the upper part of Arizona. As they got closer to Arizona, the wind started picking up. They could tell the truckers had to fight to keep their rigs on the road. Frank was glad he wasn't driving their RV; Penelope was safe at the RV campground in Vegas.

In the beginning the truckers were going the speed limit of 70 mph, but as the wind picked up they started slowing down. Because the trucks were being pushed toward the other lanes, when Aggie wanted to pass a truck, she would wait until she could pass it quickly. As they entered Nevada, they headed toward a mountain that had walls on both side of the road. It acted like a funnel for the winds. All the trucks were slowing down to 40 miles and still it was hard for the drivers to keep their rigs in one lane.

As they came off the mountain they hit the high winds. It didn't take long before the truckers and the RV drivers started pulling off the road. Aggie was driving their Jeep; she had to keep both hands on the wheel. It was bad enough to deal with the wind; but now they could see a dust storm building up in the distance. When they first saw the dust storm it was on the edge of the Valley, which looked like it was a good twenty miles away. They were both hoping that it would stay in the distance, but since they were driving in that direction the odds were against them. Aggie had caught up to another large rig that was pulling three trailers, and Aggie could tell that the driver was having a hard time keeping it in one lane. At this point she didn't feel a need to pass him. But a car from behind decided to take the chance. As the car passed Agatha and then started to pass the truck that's when it really got exciting.

The car passed the end trailer with no problem but as it was passing the second trailer the back trailers started swinging into the lane the car was in. They couldn't see the car anymore, but then the end trailers swung back into position. The car was still safe but as it continued to pass the first trailer it started to move towards the car. It looked like a snake trying to catch a mouse! But the snake lost this time the car went zooming past, just as the truck driver lost control of the rig for a few seconds. Agatha slowed down, Frank said, "Oh shit!" Then in a matter of seconds it was all over with. That was enough for the truck driver, because the next place he saw to turn off, he did. But Agatha and Frank continued toward the dust storm.

The dust storm looked like it was building up; it was darker and bigger than before. There was no place to turn off; the wind was coming straight on now. It wouldn't be long before the storm would be upon them. The road was disappearing into the storm and so were the cars in front of them. This wasn't the first time they had been in a dust storm, they knew to drive slowly, and if they saw a place to turn off they would. Then the dust storm hit, between the wind and the dust, the Jeep was hard to keep on the road, but Aggie was holding her own.

Frank saw a turn off; he told Aggie and pointed at the turn off. She started to turn into it, and just as she pulled in she spotted a car already there. She almost hit it, but she pulled off just in time, then she tried again, this time there was no car. As she stopped the Jeep, the wind and dust got stronger. All they could do is wait the storm out. Frank told Aggie, "I think this is the worst dust storm we have ever seen! You can't even see the end of the Jeep's hood, now they knew what it feels like to be in a washing machine, it's just a lot dirtier." Aggie had to agree! The dust flew around them for a little while and then the dust was gone. The wind was still blowing, but not as bad as it was.

They both started to get out of the car, to see if there was any damage to the Jeep. But the wind was to strong; as they tried to open the door the wind pushed the car door shut. Aggie suggested to Frank, "Let's wait until we get home to check out if there was any damage. Frank agreed and reminded Aggie about the time they ran into the rain storm when they were dating.

They were stationed at Ft. Hood, Texas and went to Dallas for the day and on the way back they ran into a rain storm. They found out later it was the outer edges of a tornado system. Aggie said, "Yes, I'm pretty sure the car was must cleaner after that, than the Jeep looks now! The Jeep is normally black, but now it was a light brown. Frank had to agree with her, he would have to clean the Jeep when they get back to camp. The rest of the trip was windy, but was much easier to drive in.

The next couple of days were cold and windy. Toward the end of the week, the weather started warming up and the winds finally died down. Aggie and Frank were getting RV fever (cabin fever) they decided to go out to Red Rock Canyon National Conservation Area. They had heard it had countless featured scenic desert cliffs, buttes and spectacular rock formations.

The canyon was only thirty miles away, according to the flier there are 23 different paths they could take. They decided on number 12, the Ice Box Canyon trail. They headed across the wash and up the other side towards the canyon. The trail was well defined as it leads them up the canyon for a 1/4 of a mile. Then the path headed down toward the bottom of the canyon. It was starting to warm up. Frank spotted lizards laying on the different rocks that were out crops. He guessed they were enjoying the heat from the sun. It had been cold the last few days, so he was sure they needed to heat themselves up.

From this point the trail became a path that went over and around boulders as the route continued upstream. They ended at the large ponderosa pine tree at the bottom of the canyon.

Then they headed up the path that reached the upper pool. It had been filled with the seasonal waterfall.

It was much better than the pool they had seen earlier. The pool they had found earlier looked pretty nasty. It had bugs and green icky junk in it. Frank had asked Aggie, "Would you drink that, if you had too? Aggie replied, "Maybe, but I think I would really be in need of water, it would have to be a life or death situation." It was a good thing they had carried water with them.

Further down the path they came to a wall, it looked like it was going to be tricky to get past it, but they made it. They were glad they didn't bring the dogs with them. It ended up being a three mile round trip; the dogs would have had a hard time making it. They ended the day by stopping and getting some Mexican Food, before going back to the Penelope and the dogs.

The weather was windy and cold the last week they were in Vegas, it even rained a couple of times. Both Frank and Aggie were getting restless; they were ready to get out of Vegas. During their last week in Vegas, they ended up going to a couple of small museums and to a chocolate factory, which had a cactus garden; the garden was decorated for Christmas.

With the cold mornings and the strong winds they didn't get much walking in. They didn't bring heavy coats for the winter weather. So it was pretty much just taking the girls out long enough for them to do their thing and maybe walking around the museums. The casinos were out, they were too smoky and the machines kept calling to Aggie. It was cheaper to go to the museum.

Finally it was time to leave Vegas, there was another storm coming in, with 50 mph winds and maybe a heavy rain. Aggie pointed out to Frank, "This is the same thing that happened in Bend, OR. He laughed and said, "I think the bad weather is following us! It's just taking a little while to find us. Maybe we should rent ourselves out to the states that are having drought."

It was time to break down and put everything up outside, into the Jeep. As usual the plan was to leave around 10:00, because it would be after the morning traffic and before the lunch crowd. They had done a recon a couple of days ago, of the next part of their trip. Well the first part of it anyway. They will be going to Boulder City and then head to Kingman, AZ where they will spend the night, and then go to Salome.

CHAPTER 10

Arizona adventure and discovery

Wanda and Earl have a place in Salome; they go there every winter. They have been going there for the last ten years. They had invited Frank and Aggie to come and visit them. Frank and Aggie were looking forward to spending more time with them.

Frank and Aggie had everything outside put up in record time; they wanted to get everything put up before the storm arrived. It was a good thing they did too. The wind started picking up earlier than the weather lady had reported; she was off by three hours. They had turned on the news the night before to check the weather. The weather lady said, the winds would be around 25 mph by early morning and it would be stronger as the day went on. The weather lady was right; Penelope was rocking back and forth as the wind grew stronger and stronger during the night. Frank and Agatha were glad they had packed everything up before the wind picked up. Frank really didn't want to chase down the gazebo or anything else for that matter.

It was a long night but by 3:00 am the wind had started to die down. They've both finally fell asleep, around 3:30. They slept in until 8:00 am which was a surprise to both of them. Normally, they were up by 6:00 a.m. If they weren't, the girls would be waking them up; they would need to go out to do their business.

As usual by 9:00 o'clock they were ready to go. Frank was taking the lead as usual. Because Frank said, Aggie would take off and leave him behind. She had the tendency of getting too far ahead of him.

They had decided earlier that week to do a recon of the first leg of the trip. It ended up being helpful to do a recon of the area before heading out this time. They took Hwy 93 to Boulder city; it was only fifteen miles away from Vegas. They wanted to make sure there weren't any turns that they didn't see on the map or any surprises they may need to know about. It is much easier to turn the Jeep around than it would be to turn the RV around.

During the recon they stopped and checked out the Hoover Dam Museum in Boulder City. They had lunch, and then walked around town for a while. It was good they did the recon though; they discovered they had to be in the left lane to make their turn on Hwy 93; otherwise they would have to drive their RV through downtown, which wouldn't have been a good idea. Recon stands for Reconnaissance, which is a military term for gathering information.

They left Vegas, and made it through Boulder City without any issues and continued on to Kingman, AZ. They were only going to spend one night there and then head off to the next stop. They found a Good Sam campground on the other side of Kingman which was perfect. This way they wouldn't have to deal with town traffic. It was a nice campground; it was on a hill side, not far from the highway, and close to a truck stop.

"Kingman prehistory belongs to Patayan (old ones), their culture and descendants; principally the Hualapai, Havasupai and Mohave tribes. The US Camel Corps surveyed along the 35th parallel in 1857, to establish a new road west. In 1880 Lewis Kingman surveyed for the Atlantic and Pacific Railroad, the first train pulled out of town in 1883."

There are over 60 buildings that are on the National Register of Historic Places, in Kingman. Frank and Aggie stopped at the Powerhouse Route 66 Museum, it tells the story of Route 66 (Mother Road) as it was called. There were murals, photos and life size dioramas in the museum.

Aggie and Frank found out that there were other museums in Kingman: Mohave Museum of History & Arts, which was about the Wild West and the local traditions of earlier times. The other one was Kingman Army Airfield Museum which observes the history of the Kingman Airfield Gunnery Training Base, where over 36,000 soldiers trained during WWII."

They didn't find the brochure until they went to the Powerhouse museum. But according to the brochure, there were a lot of things to do and see there. They wished they would have checked them out, but they already made plans to be in Salome tomorrow.

When they arrived at the campground outside of Kingman, there were only three rigs in the campground. By the next morning there were 30 rigs set up at the campground. It was always good to get to the campground early; that way you get the best parking area.

The lady at the front desk had told Agatha and Frank to be aware of the coyotes in the area. They were afraid that the coyotes may grab their small dogs, if they weren't careful. She said, "They have been seen close to the campground, but hadn't actually attacked anything at this point." She suggested that we don't take the dogs out on to the trails and just keep them in the dog park area, it is fenced off.

Frank and Aggie took her advice and just took the dogs to the dog park, as she suggested. Then they went over to the restaurant at the truck stop and had dinner. Another uneventful night which was nice, the wind was a little strong, but other than that it was a nice evening. They figured it will only take a couple of hours tomorrow to get to Salome.

The next morning it was pretty easy to leave the campground, they didn't have to move much around; the Jeep was still loaded from the day before. All Frank had to do is disconnect the water and electricity and Aggie had to pull in the room on the RV. She put the few items that they had pulled out during the night, back where they belonged.

Frank had gotten up first this time and made the coffee, and let the dogs out to do their business. The wind had followed them again, and the temperature was in the 30s this morning, so Agatha was glad that Frank had taken the dogs out.

Frank had been looking at the map when he said "Aggie did you realize that we have been on Hwy 93 since we left Twin Falls Idaho?" Aggie responded that she really didn't think about it much. He showed her the map, and she just smiled and said, "I'll be damn!"

They loaded up and headed down the hill and stopped at the truck stop to fill up their rigs and get more propane for the RV. They needed to follow Hwy 93 down to Hwy 71 and they would finally be off of Hwy 93 from then on. Well at least for now anyway.

The Hwy 93 was pretty much the same as the rest of the high desert and up and down a lot of hills. As they turned onto Highway 71 they entered into another Valley, this valley was called McMullen Valley. This valley was different, as they came down the mountain, they could see farm land in the distance.

The McMullen Valley is also called, "The heart of Arizona outback." As Aggie was looking at the brochure, she had found out about the area earlier that morning. It pointed out that there were many stories and history about McMullen valley. Frank and Agatha were looking forward to exploring the area with Wanda and Earl. They had told them so much about the area while they were in Bend, OR.

They arrived in Salome around noon. As they drove into Salome, there wasn't much there at first glance. There are a couple of bars and two small grocery stores, and a post office that were still running. There were many more businesses that didn't make it; they were closed up or for sale.

Aggie called Wanda to get directions to their place, as they got closer. The road they were supposed to drive down was a dirt road, instead of a paved road. Aggie wanted to make sure it was the right road before taking Penelope on it.

Aggie couldn't help thinking; cell phones were wonderful, at times like this. It was one of the conditions the kids had made to them about traveling around the country. They would carry a cell phone, and let them know each time they moved and what direction they were going. Of Course, it was also great that they could talk to the kids and grandkids, whenever they wanted to. Frank and Aggie both missed them all tremendously; they did hate missing the kid's different events in their lives. But it was something they had always wanted to do, travel around this wonderful country of ours!

When they pulled around the corner they couldn't believe how wonderful Earl and Wanda's place was! As they pulled Penelope into their lot, where they would be parking, it felt like paradise. After living in the Vegas campground, this was like a big parking lot. After three weeks, this seemed wonderful.

There was so much space; all the connections, electricity, water and sewage were all there. Earl and Wanda had a 5th wheel, which was parked in a large building. The building had a two car garage, bedroom, bathroom and a second-floor loft. Earl did all of the wood work himself, he's pretty handy with his hands when it comes to construction. Their lot had a brick wall around their property, the bricks came from Mexico, and they were unusual red, orange and yellow, very pretty. Frank and Agatha hadn't seen that type of brick before.

As Frank and Aggie set up the RV, they were again impressed at how wonderful a place it was. So much space! The view was amazing too, the mountain ranges in the distance encircled the valley, and each range had their own name and stories about them.

Another great thing was the girls got along with Wanda and Earl's dogs. They could run around their property without being on a leash, and not worrying about any other dogs attacking them. It didn't take the girls long to figure out that they could run all over the place. Well at least as long as they stayed inside of the brick walls.

Once everything was settled down, they all sat down to visit with each other. They had agreed that meals would be separate, with the exception of once in a while and they agreed that Thanksgiving would be at Wanda's. This way they wouldn't have to worry about each other's time table for eating. It makes it much easier to stay with people, if you don't intrude too much on their life.

Next couple of days Wanda and Earl showed them around town, and walked around the neighborhood. The neighborhood was under development, but the developer had to stop due to legal issues. There were about 20 sites that were all the same size property, and all the roads were paved in the area; it was nice to go for walks with the dogs.

Frank and Aggie were looking forward to walking out in the country, and not having to deal with the nightmares of Las Vegas. Earl warned them to keep an eye out for coyotes and rattlesnakes when they we're out walking. You never know when they might be around. He also told us before letting the dogs out of the RV in the morning, to check to make sure there was nothing in the yard which could hurt them.

The properties were all the same size lots, but each was different as far as the landscaping went. Some had the large building to cover their rigs, and had the brick fence around the property. They each had two gates where they could pull in the rigs and one small gate in the center with an archway they could walk through.

Each of the properties around there was different in many ways. All of the people in the neighborhood were retired. They would only come down in the winter, a few of them lived there year-round, but it was just too hot for most of them. Once it started getting They would pack up and go back north, which normally they started leaving in May.

As they walked around they saw Saguaro skeletons in people yards, they had found in the desert. The Saguaro cactus skeletons they found out in the desert were the last surviving entity of the cactus. The cactus can live upward of 150 to 200 years. As they traveled in both Nevada and Arizona they had seen many Saguaro cactuses. Usually, as they drove there would be just a few, and were small. But as they drove south, the Saguaros would increase in numbers and their size would change. There are very few Saguaros in the area, around Salome.

Anyway, some of the neighbors had orange trees and a variety of cactuses and rocks which were mostly found out in the desert or in the mountain range around them. Wanda and Earl had cactuses and rocks in their front yard of their property as decoration. Earl had told them, that the cactuses were about 6 inches high when he found them out in the desert and planted them in their yard about 10 years ago. They are now about 3 to 5 feet tall and healthy looking!

It was time to do some exploring in the area, and rock hounding, and maybe some fishing if the opportunity permitted. They packed a lunch and headed out to Lake Alamo. Frank had heard it had the best largemouth bass in Arizona. They went to the viewpoint by the damn, so they could see the whole lake. The view point was high on a ridge at eye level with the ravens and vultures; you can see the Bill Williams River, which formed the Alamo Lake.

The name Alamo comes from the Mexican word "Cottonwood tree". They could see a volcano shaped mound across the lake to the north, which is called "Artillery Peak." According to the sign at the dam, "Bill Williams was one of the more colorful mountain men who ranged over the Rocky Mountains and Southwest trapping beaver, his nickname was "Old Solitaire." Although Parker dam was finished in 1939, Alamo Lake dam wasn't completed until 1968. The lake is well known for its recreational fishing, holding the reputation as of the best largemouth bass fishing lake in Arizona."

After checking out the dam they deciding that the water was too low to go fishing, they would go rock hounding instead. As they drove along the back roads, they found larger cactuses some were over 30 feet tall with at least 15 arms on them. Many of them had bird nest in them and looked like they had a rough life. They stopped at a couple places off the road and found some unusual rocks, a smooth green stone and lots of quartz embedded into other rocks. As they went around the rim of the desert above the lake, they found another little town that was basically RVs and a little store there.

By then it was getting late so they headed back to the house to settle in for the next day. The plan was to head to Buckeye tomorrow and pick up groceries for Thanksgiving dinner. It would be a two hour drive one way, Salome did have grocery stores, but they were very small and didn't have all of the supplies they needed for a special dinner.

The next morning they headed out about 9 o'clock and went to Buckeye, to do the grocery shopping. As they were going to Buckeye, Agatha spotted a little miniature white church on the side of the road. Agatha asked Wanda what was the deal with the church in the middle of nowhere. Wanda replied, "That it was called the Little Roadside Chapel. They had different events there throughout the year and it was a very positive restful place to visit. Agatha suggested that on the way back from Buckeye, they should stop and check out the chapel.

After being out in the desert for the last couple of weeks they have been away from everyone, it was quite the change to go to Buckeye. There were people going every which way. After shopping they decided to have lunch before heading back home.

As they were returning back to Salome, they came up on the chapel and decided to go ahead and stop. There was an older lady there that was checking on the place and cleaning it up a little bit. From what we understood she was the lady that had donated the building to the City of Salome. They dedicated it to the city in 2004. The chapel was about 12' x 16' and had benches inside both sides of the chapel. It had a little podium up front and stained-glass windows.

There were three stained-glass windows on both side and there was a little steeple with a cross on top. As Aggie stood outside of the chapel she could see one Saguaro cactus to the left of it. To the right there was an area where they would have little events such as Easter sunrise service. They even had a few weddings from our understanding. It was a very peaceful and restful place to visit.

When they arrived back at the house, they unloaded all the groceries and planned for Thanksgiving dinner. Wanda would cook the turkey in their RV, and Agatha would make some of the other food in their RV. They spent the evening enjoying the night air. It was still staying warm in the evenings even for November. Tomorrow Wanda wanted to take them to a Pottery and gift shop outside of Salome, to a town called Harcuvar. Aggies said it sounded like a really cool place to go and said how about we head out there about 10 o'clock tomorrow: everyone was in agreement. They called it a night and looked forward to the next day.

The next day they went to the pottery gift shop, but it is closed on Wednesday, so all they could do is look over the fence at all of the unusual things they had. Aggie couldn't believe all the cool things that were sitting out in there. Everything was made out of metal and rocks, it was remarkable. There were peacocks, cactuses, horses, mules, colorful flowers, and other little creatures all were made out of metal plating, and welded together. It was amazing to see.

As they started to drive off Agatha spotted even more metalwork in the parking lot. There were life size horses pulling a life size coach, and another one with a horse pulling a covered wagon. There was a full sized metal man riding a horse, the mane of the horse was sticking straight up and the man even was wearing a cowboy hat. The plan was to come back later that week so they could check out all the other stuff that was in the yard. Next stop was to find petroglyphs on a rock somewhere in Harcuvar, according to a brochure.

They couldn't find it so they stopped at the Chamber of Commerce and asked if they knew where it was at and the lady that was in there had no clue about it. Wanda wanted to show us the Dick Wick Hall Monument in Salome. The Salome name means "Where she danced." According to the lady at the Chamber of Commerce, Dick was out exploring the area and decided to make it his home so he went back and got his friend and his wife to come join him. As they stopped at the edge of town they got out of the vehicle to check it out, the lady didn't have her shoes on so when she stepped out onto the sand she started jumping back and forth as if she was dancing hence the name Salome, "Where she danced!

They never did find the petroglyphs rock but they were determined they would find it sooner or later. Earl had told them about an old prison that was up in the mountain range where they would keep prisoners to quarry for the rocks, which they would use in Yuma at the territorial prison. But we would need an ATV to get up there. Earl and Wanda had taken pictures of the prison area, when they were up there checking it out. At least they could see what it looked like. This is another site that was little known and was very interesting. This was another thing that they would have to plan to go see in the future.

The next couple of days they enjoyed just hanging out in the area going for walks and hiking in the desert. Aggie started getting restless so it was time to go on another adventure, this time they were going to go to Quartzsite, Arizona.

The information they gathered about Quartzsite was "It is known as a gathering place of a different kind. In the hot summer months, it is a place where weary travelers can make a stop for food, lodging, fueling, and shopping on the way to places east, west, north and south. In the summer temperatures here get to be in the 100s and up. But it's just another sleepy town in the south in the desert during this time of year."

"In the winter months, when the temperatures are often in the 70s most of the time, the town turns into one of the biggest gatherings of people in the country. Over 1 million visitors, most of them are called "Snowbirds" because they migrate here from the northern climates, converging on Quartzsite in the winter."

Frank and Aggie went by themselves this time; Earl and Wanda had other plans. As Frank and Aggie drove into Quartzsite they noticed that the town was enclosed by several mountain ranges and had a variety of plant life in the desert. As they drove through town, they saw RV campgrounds everywhere and RV's just parked out in the desert.

The town was small; it was hard to believe that a million people come here in the winter. They drove to the other side of town where they found a rock store, and other unusual stores. They stopped at the rock store, and in front of it, it had a camel made out of tire rims wheels and other car parts, it was painted red with white legs, it stood about seven feet. They spent the afternoon walking from one store to another.

Each store was more interesting then the last one. One place had a pile of animal skulls, and other things from Russia. After a few hours of walking around, it was time to head back to Salome. Aggie told Frank, she didn't think she would want to come here when there were a million people here.

As they drove down I10 they decided to take another route home, so they took road SR72. They stopped at the truck stop to get gas, just in case they get lost, and then went the back way to Salome. The scenery was different than on Hwy 60 going to Quartzsite. There were dairy farms on both sides of the road, where on 60 it was all desert and a few small towns. It was interesting to see that the farmers had covers for the cattle and large fans to keep the cattle cool. It was kind of weird to see fans hanging from the ceiling outside. It made since, if they wanted to keep the cattle alive, otherwise they could die from the heat. There wasn't any place for the cattle to go except under the cover they had built for them.

One thing about AZ, you can't really get lost. All the roads go on grids, and there are only a few main roads, if you know them you can go anywhere. Tomorrow will be another exploding day; they planned on doing a recon to their next camp site, Cottonwood, AZ.

Earl and his brother had warned them about going over the mountain range and going through Prescott. According to the guys; there are two ways that they could by-pass mountain road, instead of taking the old mountain road. There is three different ways to go to Cottonwood, and they were going to check out two of them tomorrow.

They started out early; they took Hwy 60, and then 71, then 89. When they got to Kirkland Junction, they had to choose which way to go, either over the mountain or around it. They chose to take the mountain on!

They turned onto 89 and headed up the mountain. Almost immediately they started to climb. They could see the road ahead; it looked like a long snake, going back and forth. At one point there was a sign that said, "No vehicles over 40 feet long" their rig was 30 ft. long." They were glad they were driving the Jeep, instead of having the RV. As they continue to go up the mountain, it became a two lane road with no passing. If you looked of out the passenger side you could see the valley below, for hundreds of miles. As they got closer to the top, they stopped and took a couple of pictures. They wanted to show the kids. The kids wouldn't believe how beautiful it was up there. You could see one mountain range after another, most covered with trees. There were small towns throughout the drive.

As they headed down the mountain, their view changed from mountain range to forest, with large pine trees. It was hard to believe they were in Arizona. They finally reached Prescott, which is a larger older town on Hwy 89; 89 went right thought the old part of town. The old courthouse and older businesses were on the main road.

They didn't stop there; they came down into the Prescott Valley, and got on I10. After that they ended up climbing up and down hills for the rest of the drive to Cottonwood. Aggie told Frank they should come back after they settled in at Cottonwood. He agreed, "Hopefully it won't snow before we do! Winter is on its way."

Two hours later they were in Cottonwood, they checked out the campground and both agreed they wouldn't be taking Penelope over the mountain range.

After lunch they decided to take the freeway back, after an hour and half they were back in Salome. It was much nicer taking the freeway back. It was a longer way around, but it was much faster than going over the mountain on the back road.

After a three week visit, it was time to leave Salome, and head to Cottonwood. They had no intention of going over the mountain via Prescott, with the RV. Even if it would have saved 30 miles, it would have taken a lot more gas and time to climb over the mountain, because they would have to go slower and Penelope would have had to work twice as hard.

Even in the Jeep they couldn't go much faster than 35 to 45 miles an hour. But it was a beautiful place to go for a drive.

They took Hwy 60 to the outskirts of Phoenix and then Interstate 17 to Cottonwood. It was a nice trip, a little on the boring side as far as Aggie was concerned. Aggie realized this was the first time they have been on a freeway with Penelope since with Nampa, Idaho. Of course she had to call Frank on the radio and tell him, all he said was "Really!" The only stop they made was at a rest stop, it was called Sunset View, it was great, and the view was beautiful. Aggie could only imagine what the sunset would be like. They had left around 9:30 and arrived about three hours later at Verde Valley campground.

Frank and Aggie had stopped there about 15 years ago when they had been traveling with her parents. At that time, it was a small campground, it was beautiful and clean. It was close to the Verde River and there was lots of wildlife to watch. There were all kinds of quail, rabbits, chipmunks, eagles and even a few javelins. They could even hear coyotes at night in the distance.

But now everything had changed, it was three times as big and people permanently were living on some sites now. It now had three sections to choose from. During the recon earlier that week they had already decided on going to the farthest site they had. There were not that many people and it was the smallest section of the campground. They enjoyed being away from crowds and hopefully see wildlife coming through. After all those years on the island, it was still hard for them to be around large groups.

After Frank and Aggie had set up camp they walked around the campground, they wanted to figure out where they had parked 16 years ago. Everything had changed; they could hear the river through the trees, but couldn't see it now. Before, they could see the river and walk down to it, but now the trees and brush have taken over that part of the land. Frank told Aggie this sure isn't what I remember, Aggie had to agree with him. They finished walking the girls and called it a night and settled in and watched some TV.

The next couple of days they drove around and checked out the visitor center in Camp Verde. Camp Verde is a town, not a military post. But they do have an old military post outside of their town. It is Fort Verde, according to the brochure, "General Cooks U.S. Army scouts and soldiers were primarily posted at Fort Verde in the 1870s and 1880s. From 1865-1891 Camp Lincoln, Camp Verde and Fort Verde were home to officers, doctors, families, enlisted men, and scouts."

The park ranger told them, "The Park is the best-preserved example of an Indian Wars period fort in Arizona. Several of the original buildings still stand and are living history. They have programs that are scheduled periodically; it gives the visitors a glimpse into Arizona's history. The soldiers were given the task of preventing Apache and Yavapai Indian uprising."

Frank and Agatha wandered around the museum, which used to be the old headquarters building. They were amazed at all the items that were on display, from that time. The museum even had period clothing from the 1880's. The ranger told Frank and Aggie they could get dressed up in the period clothing and have their picture taken. Of course, Frank and Agatha had to dress up and get their picture taken. Frank put on a blue army officer cavalry over coat, and old black cavalry hat. Aggie put on an old time pioneer dress, which went all the way down to the floor, and to finish it off she put on an old straw hat. What a couple!

One room was dedicated to the history about the Indian Scouts and Indian war errs. They even had interviews from some of the Indians family members that were scouts or warriors during that time span. It was interesting to hear the other side of the Indian wars.

After the museum, they wandered over to where there were three old military buildings, which were the officer quarters at one time. They were all furnished in the 1880s period. As they wandered from one building to the next it was amazing how they felt. They felted like they were living life through the eyes of the soldiers and their family members. The houses were decorated with original furniture and toys. They could only imagine what it was like to live in that time.

It was a cold day when they walked through the houses, so it was understandable why they had fireplaces in each of the rooms. The houses were pretty large and had two floors; there were many more buildings at one time. But though the year's people would come in and take the wood and use it for their houses and furniture.

The Ranger on duty was great; you could tell she enjoyed being there. She said, "They have reenactments during the year, and they even buried a time capsule at the camp. They dressed in the period dress, during the ceremony.

After they were back in the car, Frank wanted to see the pictures they had taken earlier of them in the period clothes. He started laughing and told Aggie, "You look like Ma Kettle!" Aggie looked at the picture and laughed. She said, "Your right!" After visiting the fort, they went downtown to Camp Verde and visited the other shops and had lunch at a local Mexican restaurant.

The Ranger gave them a map, which had all the different points of interest in the area, all within a thirty mile radius. Frank and Agatha decided to head out first thing in the morning and see how many of the interest points they could see. They were going to start at Montezuma Castle National Monument, then Montezuma Well, next stop would be the

V BarV petroglyphs site. There was going to be some hiking trails they could take so they decided to take the dogs and a picnic lunch.

The next morning they were up and ready to go by 9 o'clock, first stop Montezuma Castle. Montezuma Castle was built by the Southern Sinagua Indian farmers. It was built five-stories high, and was a 20-room dwelling; they think it was sometime built between 1100 and 1300. The cliff recess is 100 feet above the valley. Early American settlers marveled at the structure, they assumed that it was the Aztecs who were the original owners, hence the name Montezuma Castle.

As they checked in to the visitor center, (which was free), they looked at all of the artifacts that were on display. Then they headed up the path to see Montezuma Castle. You could see the castle at the top of the cliff, from the visitor center. Pictures just don't do it justice; they wondered how they managed to get up and down into the fortress. They could only imagine what it looked like in their time. They had to use ladders to go up and down into their home. Carrying all the food and water up and down or passing it from one person to another.

Next stop was Montezuma Well, they really weren't sure if they wanted to go see it. They just assumed it was a small hole in the ground, but what the heck they thought they might as well go check it out. It wasn't that far from Montezuma Castle anyway. As they drove over to the next site, Agatha read the information from the flyer. According to the flyer they got from the ranger: "Montezuma Well" has lush vegetation in the midst of the desert. It is a limestone sink hole formed long ago, still fed by continuous flowing springs.

The Southern Sinagua irrigated crops with the water; you can still see traces of lime-coated irrigation ditches. The pit house built inside the hole on top is dated around 1050 AD. The Southern Sinagua building around here ranged in size from one room houses to large Pueblos. They lived there between 1125 thought 1400 and there was about 100-250 people that lived there."

It was a short drive from Montezuma Castle, the girls had to stay in the car, pets are not allowed on the site. It was a cool day, around 55 degrees, so they would be ok in the car. As they walked down the path, they could see large old cottonwood trees. The area was located at the edge of the desert. There was grass and small trees. They headed to the Visit Center, where a volunteer ranger was waiting to help them.

One of the first information signboards at the lake explained it all, "In a region where water is sacred, Montezuma Well water rises from deep underground and flows constantly. It is known and used by people throughout time and it is a sacred landscape to this day by the people in the area.

Montezuma Well is a holy place of emergence in some tribal histories. It is called Yuvukva (sunken spring) and Tawapa (sun spring) by the Hopi, Ah-hah-gkith-gygy-vah (broken water) by the Yavapai, and Tu sii che'IL (water breaks open) by the Western Apache.

Frank told Aggie, "That any of the traditional names for the Well make more scene than Montezuma. The Aztec emperor lived long after the sites had been occupied and far to the south in Old Mexico."

Aggie had moved on to another sign, where it talked about the things that lived in the wells water. There are fresh water leeches, ducks, and turtles, but no fish. Aggie had to wonder, how did the leeches and turtles get there? She asked Frank, could you imagine finding this well, after being lost in the desert and just jumping into it, then coming up out of the water and having leeches all over your body. What a nightmare! Frank laughed, and said, I'll bet they would be running back out into the desert!

As they continued to follow the hiking trail, they came down the hill, there was another ruin, but the sign board had been destroyed. Frank and Aggie both wondered why anyone would do this. The next few sign boards were damaged too, all Frank would say was, "Idiots."

They followed the trail back to the parking lot. It was a good thing too, the girls were getting tired. There was another site they wanted to stop at before going to the V Bar V Ranch. It was called a pit house. They left the girls in the car, and got no complaints from the girls. They wouldn't be gone very long, maybe 10 minutes. They opened the windows in the car, just a little bit, and then went over to the site. According to the sign board, "The Pit house was built between 600 and 1400 AD. The pit that Frank and Aggie were looking at was dated to 1050 AD; it was used by farming families' tribes."

The National Park Association restored the area by covering the pit and added a wall to protect the hole. They had cleaned it up and built a cover to protect it from anymore damage. Inside the covered area there were holes in a circle and lines, it had a red rock floor, and there were two large holes which were used to hold the roof up. According to the sign, "The holes around the edge revealed the outline of the structure, where the wall posts were placed in the ground. The biggest hole was used for a fire pit. They had a picture which was a cutaway view of the structural; it showed what it would have looked like, in its day.

As they headed back to the car, they both wondered how they could live in the desert in the summer. It was in the 70's already, and there was no shade around there.

As they approached the car, the girls started barking. Aggie opened the door to the Jeep and Susie jumped out, and didn't stop until she found a bush. Aggie told Frank, "I guess she had to go!" Frank just laughed and called Susie; they let Sheba out too, and walked them for a little while, then loaded up, next stop V Bar V Ranch.

"V Bar V Heritage site has the largest known petroglyphs site in the Verde Valley of Central Arizona, and one of the best preserved. The rock art site consists of 1032 petroglyphs in 13 panels. Petroglyphs are images created by removing part of a rock surface by incising, picking, carving or abrading, as a form of rock art."

It sound like it was an interesting place to visits. As they walked toward the visitor center; there stood an old fireplace and chimney. They guessed it use to be part of the ranch house, on the property.

After checking into the visitor center, they headed down a path that leads to the petroglyphs. On the way there, there we're huge cottonwoods and even a few deer. The deer must have been use to seeing people; they just looked up at them, and then went back to eating. As they reached the site, they were surprised how many people were already there. They even had a ranger to answer questions and tell everyone a little history about the area. The petroglyphs had fencing around it to protect it from being vandalized, like they did at the other sites. It was so peaceful out there; all you could hear was the creek and the birds singing. After taking a lot of pictures and listening to the ranger they headed back to the Jeep.

As they were walking back to the Jeep, Aggie told Frank she was going to make a list of everything to do in the area, which is called the Verde Valley. She had no idea how many things there are to do until she started making the list; it's kind of like the RV list she started in Bend, and gave up on.

The next day they headed off in a different direction, they were going to go to another Indian ruin, called Tuzigoot, and then the Clemenceau Heritage Museum, Clarkdale Museum and end the day at Copper Art Museum.

They walked into the welcome center at Tuzigoot, and signed in. It had artifacts from the Southern Sinagua village. Afterwards they headed up to the ruins. It was quite large; they did a great job of restoring it. As they walked up the trail, they read the signs and looked at the amazing view.

Every ruin they have been to always have a great view. But Aggie was pretty sure that's not why they built the village on top of the hill. The walls were high and they entered from the top of the building. The ladders were made out of small trees roped together with some kind of twine. According to the information they had received, "Tuzigoot (Apache for "Crooked water") is the remnant of a Southern Sinagua village built between 1000 and 1400 AD. It crowns the summit of a long ridge rising 120 feet above the Verde Valley. The original pueblo was two stories high in places, with 87 ground-floor rooms.

There were few exterior doors; entry was by ladders through roof openings. The village began as a small cluster of rooms inhabited by some 50 persons for about 100 years. In the 1200s the population doubled and then doubled again."

Of course they climbed down into the rooms below. They looked a lot larger inside of the room than outside. There was a display in the room showing where they cooked and slept. As they climb up to the roof it was obvious why they picked this place. There was no way anyone could sneak up on them, and there was water, plants and animals close at hand. Aggie as usual could imagine how they must have lived. She could imagine them climbing up and down the hill to get food and water. Just to keep the family alive and healthy.

Next stop Clemenceau Heritage Museum, as they arrived at the Museum, they could tell it must have been a school at one time. They were met by an older gentleman, who volunteered to show people around. It's always nice to have a guide. As they were being shown around, the gentlemen explained that the museum had been a school house at one time. So there is one room that is a permanent schoolroom from that time. In the other rooms they had early 20th century home interiors, and artifacts from that time.

Frank's favorite part was the model train room. It showed the different layers, from the mining, smelting and cattle ranching life during that time period. There were at least ten trains running in the display. One would disappear and another would come out a tunnel. It was a model railroad of the 1895-1953 eras with replica steam locomotive and ore cars. They had little town's replicas of Clarkdale, Clemenceau, Old town Cottonwood and Jerome. It was very cool and it was amazing how much detail they had in the display.

Next stop was the Copper Art Museum in Clarkdale, as they drove up to the museum the first thing they saw was a huge copper kettle on display in front of the museum, as they drove around the corner there were old ore car with copper ore loaded in them. Aggie had to check that out, they were all cemented into the car. As they entered the museum, they saw copper footprints on the floor. The lady at window welcomed them, she told them to just follow the copper foot prints, so they did. How cool!

They found room after room of incredible art and displays of different exhibits going all the way back to Roman times, all made out of copper. Then they entered the Military Art Room, inside it had Trench Art, the walls were lined with Artillery Shell Casings, each one had different carvings on them. The ones on display were collected from WW I Western Front trenches warfare. The soldiers would have time on their hands and started carving on the shells. There was a sign that explained who, when and where.

There was so much to see, there were collections of Kitchenware, Drink ware Collections and display of Art and Architecture. The Distillery and Winery display were amazing. It took a couple of hours to go thought the museum; there was so much to see and such beautiful art pieces. Well Aggie thought to herself, we have a few more things to check off our list.

After finishing her list, she started checking everything they had been too. It looks like they still have a lot to see, and there was a lot more to see than what was on her list. They're just going to have to come back, their next stop is Tucson, and then to Benson, AZ.

Things to do in Cottonwood, AZ

Fort Verde	X	Cottonwood Historical	X	Dead Horse Ranch State Park	X
Camp Verde	X	Clarkdale Historical town		Red Rock State Park	X
Montezuma Castle	X	Jerome Historical town	X	Jerome State Park	X
Lake Montezuma		Verde Canyon Railroad		Slide Rock State Park	X
Montezuma Well	X	Palatki Heritage site		Oak Creek Canyon	X
VBarV Petroglyphs Site	X	Clemenceau Heritage Museum	X	Clarkdale Museum	X
Tuzigoot Nat'l Monument	X	Copper Art Museum	X	Sedona	X
Honanki Heritage Site		Homolovi Ruins State Park		Lots of hiking trails	

The trip to Tucson didn't take long; they stayed at a 55 and over campground. It had everything; it was very different from all of the other places they had stayed. It was more of a community with people living in different types of homes, from RV to cabins to mobile homes. It even had a hotel, three pools and many other things. It had security guards, and no one got into the place without an ID card, or security code. It was nice, but it wasn't for Frank and Aggie, they liked their campgrounds a little more out in the country.

They stayed a week during that time. The first two days it was in the 40s and windy. Then for three days it rained, the roads were flooding, and the parking area had at least two inches of water. The dog park was under water, it was a wash during the raining season. Aggie thought to herself, she would hate to be at the end of the wash, where the water stops. On Wednesday it was time to head to Benson, which was thirty miles east; they had checked it out earlier on the internet and made a reservation.

As usual it was raining when it was time to go, and then it started to snow on the way to Benson. They were both glad it would be a short drive today. Frank couldn't believe the idiot drivers on the road. The speed limit is 75 on the freeway, and even with the snow storm they are still going 75 and faster. Within the three miles they saw five car accidents, most were people going off the road, just before they reached Benson there was a five car accident on the other side of the freeway. The police were there and the cars were already backed up for a mile. As the snow continued to fall and the wind was picking up, they felt sorry for the people that were stuck on the other side, but really happy it didn't happen on their side.

They arrived in Benson campground around two, and set up camp. They only did what had to be done; it was supposed to be nice tomorrow. The next morning the snow was all gone; there was three inches on the ground when they parked yesterday. Once everything was set up they did a "Walk about!" It wasn't anything like the Tucson campground. But it was cheaper and friendly, it was called Vista Valley RV Resort. It wasn't too busy; they had Frank and Aggie park their rig at the far side of the campground. The desert was behind them and two other rigs, one on each side and a few spaces away. It was nice not having people parked right next to them. The first morning Aggie could watch the sun rise from the bedroom window.

"Benson was founded in 1880 prior to Arizona's mining boom; it was developed as a stopping point for the Butterfield Overland Stage. The Southern Pacific Railroad came into Benson and was there until it was purchased by Union Pacific Railroad in 1997." It's in a great location, it about 20 to 30 miles from all kinds of things to visit.

The next day Frank wanted to go Ft. Huachuca, it was about 40 miles away from Benson where they were camping at. They walked the girls and opened up the windows in the RV to keep it cool inside; it was supposed to be in the 60's. The park host gave them a list of things to do in the area. Needless to say Aggie found a place on the way that she wanted to check out. It was called Snake art and craft store. It didn't look like it was too far from Tombstone and it was on the way to Ft. Huachuca.

It was in a town called Gleason, according to the directions it was 15 miles out in the middle of nowhere. They did finally find the town, but the only thing left was a couple of old homes and a jailhouse. There was no snake store; it looked like they were restoring the jailhouse for whatever reason. It was time to get on to Ft. Huachuca.

Ft. Huachuca is an Army post that is still active, but it does have a historical history. It was set up as a camp in March 1877 for the 6th U.S. Cavalry, and became a permanent post in 1880s. It still has most of the original buildings from the old post, some are still being used.

They arrived at Ft. Huachuca around 2 pm, as they approached the front gate they were asked to go to the far left lane. The MP (military police) informed them that they had been chosen to have their car searched. The MP asked Frank and Agatha for their ID, and asked them to turn off their car and step out of their vehicle. Frank and Agatha handed them their ID, Agatha gave them her driver's license and Frank gave the female officer his retired military ID. Aggie turned off the car and got out of the vehicle with Frank and as they were doing that a security guard stood in front of the vehicle. I guess he thought maybe they would jump in and take off who knows! Then the MP asked, Aggie to open all the doors and stand away from the vehicle. Aggie followed her instructions, and then she walked over to Frank and waited.

In the beginning Aggie had no problem, then a security guard come up to her and told her the reason for the search was because she didn't have a military ID. Aggie told him that she did have a military ID but it was expired. Aggie handed it to the security guard and he promptly told her, "I'm going to have to confiscate this because it is expired and belongs to the government." Aggie was surprised, and told him that this is why they were there, too turn in the old one and get a new one. She knew she needed 2 pieces of ID to get a new military ID and she was going to use the expired card as one of her IDs. She explained that to the security guard and he said I can't give it back to you sorry. After being treated like criminals they finally were told them they had to go get a pass from the guardhouse, if they wanted to come into the post.

Frank wasn't too happy with the whole thing, but they went ahead and went over to the building and got the pass to go into the post. They went over to the administration office to get Aggies's ID, and they were told they had to make an appointment and to go down the hallway to room 10. When they found room 10, it had a sign on it that said "Moved to room 4." They walked down to room 4 and were told that they could not get an appointment until the next day. Everyone in the office looked like they could care less about anything. There was no point in trying to get in today. They set up the appointment for the next day and Aggie was wondering where all the military people were, all she saw was civilians. As they were walking out of the building Frank told Aggie, "Man this place is so screwed up." Aggie had to agree, as they walked back to the car. The military and civilian service really had changed since they had been part of that world.

They really didn't want to make another trip back, but Aggie needed to get her ID card updated. That night Aggie looked up online and found brochure about things that are in the area. If they were going to have to make the trip again, she was going visit anything she could. Their appointment was early in the morning, so they would have all day to check out things in the area. Aggie also found a shorter route to go to Ft. Huachuca; it would save them twenty miles.

They were out on the road by 7:30. The visit to Ft. Huachuca was much nicer this time around. They still had their passes from the day before, so they went right thought the gate, and they arrived 45 minutes early. They figured they would have to wait until their appointment. At first the lady come out and told them they were early and they had to wait. Then another lady came out and told them to come on in, there was no point in having them wait until their appointment. It took all of ten minute and Aggie now had legal military ID card!

Frank likes to visit the different military posts as they travel. Otherwise Aggie never would use the ID. They drove around the post and walked around the PX. Aggie was ready to do some exploring at the ghost town she had found last night. It was called Fairbank Historic Town site.

Fairbank was on their way back to camp and a short distance from Ft Huachuca. When they arrived at the site, the caretaker was working by the gate, he told them about the town and the cemetery up on the hill.

According to the brochure that they received, "Fairbank was an old West railroad town, founded in 1882 during the

Tombstone silver boom. From 1882 to 1903, Fairbank was tombstones train depot. The town had an elegant hotel, with a restaurant and bar, a post office, several businesses and a school. Chinese farmers raised crops along the river." Now all that was left was a train depot, school and a bunch of dilapidated buildings. The cemetery was over a half mile away.

Frank and Agatha decided to head up to the cemetery to check out what was there. They always found it interesting to visit old cemeteries you can find out more about the people that lived in the town than the records that people use to keep.

As they walked up the trail to the cemetery, (it was a half mile walk from the town center), there was mesquite trees and brush along the way. There were old medal parts and an old rock foundation on the trail up to the cemetery. It was quite a climb and a narrow path to the top. Frank had to wonder how they bought the bodies up to the top of the hill to bury them. It didn't look like there was any road going up the hill, just a small path that they had walked on earlier. When they reached the top of the hill it offered majestic views of the valley.

Once they arrived at the cemetery, they were surprised how badly it was maintained. They could tell where each of the graves in the cemetery were, they are marked by piles of rocks and stones. There were a few weathered wooden crosses that still distinguished some of the grave sites too. But none of them had names on the crosses. It was sad how the people that were buried there were pretty much forgotten. There were a few of the burial sites that had iron fencing shielding the early settler's final resting spot, at one time. A few of the grave sites use to have wooden fencing around them; they now lay on top of the graves. The cemetery had a strange, lonely feeling to it. Most of engraving or writing on the grave markers has faded into history.

The one that got Aggies attention was the one that had a stuffed teddy bear, and lots of little toys. It had a wooden cross lying on top of the grave. It had to be an old grave, but yet the teddy bear just sits there looking after the little boy's grave. The reason she thought it was a boy is because the little toys were dinosaurs, army men, a lizard and a couple of horses.

As they were leaving Aggie asked Frank, "Did you feel any sprits?" He told her, "No, everyone had left a long time ago. As they headed back down the hill, they came across a couple of deer. The deer looked at each other and then looked at Frank and Agatha, then continued to eat. Aggie just smiled at Frank, and told him she guessed the deer didn't think they were much of a threat to them.

After a little bit they had walked back to Fairbanks, and they walked around the town, checking out the buildings that were left standing. There were information signs in different areas of the town, which had pictures of the townspeople. Aggie asked Frank, "How many of these people do you think are buried on top of that hill?" Frank replied "Maybe all of them!"

It didn't take long to get home. As soon as they opened the RV door; the girls were ready to go for a walk. After their walk they wanted to be fed! While Frank made the girls dinner, Aggie made theirs. They settled in for the night, it's been getting down in the 20s again. They had to bring in the plants and open the grey water tank. Frank had bought some insulation to put on the water hose and the new water filter system they had purchased earlier that week.

They would let the water drip in the bathroom sink to ensure that the water wouldn't freeze in the RV. This has been part of their nightly routine every night since Cottonwood. It may be nice and warm during the day, but the nights could get down into the teens.

According to the weather man it was going to be in the low 20's and high 50s this week. The next few days were windy and in the low 50's, so the weather man was off on the high 50s, but he was right about the nights. Frank and Aggie didn't do much walking; it was just too cold with the wind blowing. Aggie started feeling kind of crappie, she ended up with a cough and feeling really tired. For the next couple of days they ended up hanging around the RV. After a few days Aggie was feeling better and getting cabin fever. It was time to go on another adventure; they decided to go Ft. Bowie. It sounded like an interesting place to go and there was lots of history in the area.

The next morning they headed out around 9 a.m. They packed a lunch and the girls. They headed east on I10 for 22 miles, and were going to take AZ186, and from there take a road that would take them to Ft. Bowie. As they were driving down 186, Aggie spotted an old cemetery on the side of the road. They liked checking out old cemeteries, this one was called Dos Cabezas Pioneer Cemetery.

As they approached the cemetery they noticed that the gate lock was unusual. It was a ring that slipped through a slot in an iron rod, which was about 3 inches long, you push the ring up and it would open the gate. The next thing they noticed was that there were large slabs of cement on many of the graves sites. Some of the headstones were beautiful; there was one that showed the mountain range from the area. It was done in white and another memorial marker that was a circle, it had two large concrete cowboy boots, laying on their side protruding out of it about 2 inches high, with the brand of his ranch. There were a couple of sections that were fenced off for families. The oldest grave that they found, the person was buried in 1921.

The view around the cemetery was beautiful. It had mountain ranges on one side and prairie on the other. There was a fence all the way around it. Aggie assumed it was to keep the cattle and other animals out. It looked like the cemetery still was being used because there were fake flowers on some of the graves.

They loaded back up in the car and headed towards Ft. Bowie. According to the directions they had to turn on a gravel road which then turned into a dirt road and then it turned back into a paved road. As they climbed up and down the hills they stopped at one of the historical markers. The historical marker was the spot where there was a wagon train massacre. It had a sign posted telling the story about what happened. Fourteen people were killed by the Apaches and then the soldiers retaliated by catching them and hanging them. It was one of many places in that area that both sides were killed.

They stopped at the trailhead and found out that it was a mile and a half hike one way to the Fort. The sign said to plan on two hours. As they walked down the first hill and back up another hill, Sheba was already done walking. Aggie picked her up and continued on their way. The land gradually was rising and falling, there were grassy hills with bushy oak bush patches and a few rocky outcrops in the distance. The path first crosses a wash, on the other side there was a stone foundation of a mining cabin from 1860s. It was nestled in between some trees. As they continued to walk they entered a clump of trees around a smaller drainage, then they emerged into a wide valley. They arrived at the next ruins; it was the ruins of the Butterfield Overland Mail Station. It was the actual stage route that went south. You could see the tracks in the sandstones.

As they followed the path they came to the Ft. Bowie Cemetery. It was enclosed in a picket fence; it replaced the adobe wall that once surrounded it. There were 25 graves, according to the sign they were replica headstones, they had removed the bodies long ago.

From there the path turned east, they stopped in the wash and took a break. The walk was harder than they thought it would be. About that time a ranger came down the path. Aggie asked him how much farther, he told her about another ½ mile. Aggie told him, they were surprised how hard the hike has been. He told her, it's no surprise, you're up 5000 ft. Aggie told Frank, no wonder it's taking us so long. As they headed down the path, there was a small partly reconstructed adobe building and a little farther there was a replica of an Apache dwelling, called a Wiki Up.

The last section of the trip there was a wooded area that leads to Apache Spring; it still had water in it. It didn't take long before the girls were in the creek drinking and enjoying the cold water, though it was only two inches deep. Sheba would walk down stream and the mud would come swirling up, she would start to drink but didn't like the muddied water. So she would move on, and do it all over again. Frank picked her up and put her down away from the muddy water. I guess that worked for her, she stood there and drank the water. The ranger they had talked to earlier was on his way back to the ranger office. After talking to him for a little while, he told them if they need a ride back to their car, he could take them. Frank said, "That would be great." Neither one of them wanted to walk back to the car.

The trees faded away just above the spring as the trail climbs slightly to the fort, where the main complex lies straight ahead, spread over 15 acres. As they looked to the right there was the Fort Apache, it was a temporary fort until Ft. Bowie was established.

They finally made it to Ft. Bowie, it must have been a large complex at one time, and it was a site to see. As they were walking toward the ranger station, they saw the young ranger they had talked to earlier, waving his hands at the side of his head like antlers and pointing to something to the left of them. At first they thought he was waving at someone else. But there was no one else by them. Then Aggie spotted what he was waving about. There was a herd of white tail deer walking about 20 feet away from them. The deer were beautiful; again they acted like they really didn't care about them being there, as they watched the deer walk away.

Frank and Aggie were ready to take a break, trying to keep up with Susi and climbing up and down hills did them in. As they walked up to the ranger/gift shop, they could see more abode walls of the Fort. They could only imagine how hard it was to live out there. There were mountains on three sides, and a steep hike down to the water and the valley below. But it was beautiful, there was Rocky ledges harboring a varied selection of desert plants including ocotillo, cane cholla, pink flower hedgehog cactus, Arizona barrel cactus, soap tree yucca, banana yucca and Palmer's agave. The only reason they knew what the plants were was because they had signs by the plants on the trail.

According to the ranger and brochure they gave them, "On the far side of the ridge the path descends slowly via some too-gentle switchbacks, crosses a valley (Siphon Canyon) and rejoins the entrance path just north of Butterfield Mail Station, half a mile from the trailhead on Apache Pass Road." Aggie was pretty sure that was not why they build the fort here. Frank and Aggie was going to get a ride back to the Jeep, so they wouldn't get to enjoy the trail back.

The Ranger they had talked to earlier was the one that was going to take them to their car. It was a lot farther than they thought it would be they were both really glad they were going to get a ride back. Another gentlemen came down the path about fifteen minutes before they were going to leave, he had left his wife back at the car. He told us he didn't think it would take that long to walk.

What was interesting was the military occupied the Fort until 1894 and it wasn't completely abandoned until 1910. "The residents in the nearby towns removed much of the timber and some lived at the Fort off and on for a few years. "The largest area of adobe is along the walls of the cavalry barracks, on the east side of the fort. Buildings to the south were the officers quarters and the hospital, while to the west are various service structures including the general store, adjutant's office, kitchen, school, telegraph office and storeroom. The parade ground in the center still has a (replica) flagpole carrying the American flag on a 60 foot pole. The buildings on the north side are a granary, bakery, guardhouse, more barracks and storehouse, and beyond that lay the corrals and stables."

The Ranger that toke them to the Jeep was an interesting fellow. He was a young guy, and he must have been in his middle 20's. He told them he worked in different National Parks in Arizona during the winter and goes up to Alaska in the summer.

Frank and Aggie had planned to stop at Amerind Museum & Art Gallery on the way back to the RV. According to the brochure it is the "World class private collection of Native American art and artifacts from the entire western hemisphere. It was founded in 1937; it has a spectacular collection of prehistoric objects from archaeological excavations in the Americas. It also has recent items from Native cultures since the time of the first Europeans."

As they drove up the road they spotted a cemetery on the right. It was called Texas Canyon Pioneer Cemetery. Aggie suggested to Frank that they stop there on the way back. Frank replied, "Sounds like a plan."

They drove another half mile and arrived at the Museum. It was a pretty nice place; there were older buildings around it, but the two main buildings had large wooden doors that came from Old Mexico. They had to be fourteen feet high, hand carved oak. There was a smaller door that they had to go through, which both were glad to see. They weren't looking forward to pulling open those doors. They were hundreds of years old and came from an old Spanish Mission.

The museum was wonderful; it consisted of two floors, with five rooms. Each of the rooms had exhibits of different tribes and one room had ancient pottery that was donated to the museum by Mata Ortiz. She had been collecting the artifacts her whole life.

There was pottery that came from different tribes, and they are still making pottery today. After they checked out all the rooms, they went over to the art gallery. The art room was beautiful, and gave off positive energy. It was getting late and they still wanted to stop at the cemetery.

Texas Canyon Pioneer Cemetery started out as a family cemetery. The first person to be buried there was Ethel Adams, their five year old daughter. She had died after being thrown from a horse, and she was buried on January 27, 1911. This cemetery was maintained, but this one didn't have cement slabs on the graves, just head stones. It was fenced off and a different area was marked off for each family. Frank saw an unusual foundation in the middle of the cemetery. It had three large rock slabs standing on their side, and then some kind of filler and then another large slab. It didn't look like a house foundation; it ran for about a hundred feet, and then turned toward the rocks outside of the cemetery. It did not seem to have a function. It didn't look like a natural feature. "Very curious, indeed," Frank thinking to himself.

As they walked back to the car, they stopped to read the sign by the gate. It had a little history about the area, but they both thought this was interesting. According to the sign, "Reservations for burial sites made during Will Adams' time are still in effect, but no additional reservations can be made and no one can be interred here unless their name appears on the pioneer list." Another interesting thing was Texas Canyon was named because so many Texans started settling in the area, people referred to the area as Texas Canyon and it stuck.

After hanging around the campground for a few days, it was time to go on another excursion. This time they were going to Kartchner Caverns, which was outside of Benson. They arrived early to the site, so they had time to look at the display and watch a movie about the history of the cavern. It was interesting, how the cavern was discovered.

It was discovered by two guys, Gary and Randy in November 1974. Their pastime was exploring caverns and caves. This time it was the limestone hills at the eastern base of the Whetstone Mountains. The story goes, "They suspected there was a cavern there because when the rode a horse over the dome of the hill, it rang like a bell. They were looking for a cave no one had ever found.

The two kept the cave a secret until February 1978 when they told the property owners, James and Lois Kartchner, about their awesome discovery. Since unprotected caves can be seriously damaged by unregulated use, they knew the cave had to be protected."

"Gary and Randy spent several years looking into the possibility of developing the cave themselves. It wasn't until February 1978 that they told the property owners, James and Lois Kartchner, about their amazing discovery. During the four years of secret exploration, the discoverers realized that the cave's extraordinary variety of colors and formations must be preserved. The cave's existence became public knowledge in 1988."

Frank and Aggie checked into the front desk in the Visitor Center. The Ranger asked them, "Which tour do they want to go on?" Aggie was surprised that there were two different tours; they decide to go on the "Big Room Tour." It was a ½ mile and will take 1 ¾ hours. Frank looked at Aggie and told her, "We should have eaten before we came!" Aggie laughed and had to agree.

They had 45 minutes to kill before they could go on the tour. The museum had artifacts they had found in the cavern, they had found a variety of bones, which were all on display. It had pictures of the formation inside of the caverns; it was interesting to see them in the light. Normally, it is dark in the caverns, so you really can't get a good look at the formation. After that, they went to watch the movie about how the discovery happened, and what happened after the discovery was reported to the state.

Their tour was at 12:45, so as soon as the movie was over they headed over to the area they were supposed to meet the Ranger. When they arrived the Ranger was already explaining the rules and about the trip into the cavern.

They loaded up into the little train car, it was a short ride and it was cold going to the cavern. It was in the 40's outside and the wind was blowing, they both we're happy they had their heavier coats on. The Ranger explained, "The cave has an average temperature of 72° Fahrenheit (22° Celsius) and 99%

humidity year-round." The Big Room tour is only open from mid-October to mid-April, because of the bat colonies that are in the cavern. They come back every year to have their babies. That end of the cavern will stay closed until the first time the babies fly out with the colony.

The train arrived at the entrance to the cavern, which was about quarter mile from the center. Everyone unloaded from the train and headed into the cavern door, they entered into a long hallway/room, and it was about twelve feet across. The entrance way was closed behind them.

The Ranger told them, "This is the time to take off your coats and sun glasses. It wasn't hard to understand why; it was nice and warm inside the room, compared to the outside where it was cold and windy. She gave them two options; either roll their coat up and tie it around their waste or tuck it under their arm. She explained it is a live cave, and anything that they brought in could damage the cave. As far as the sunglasses, she said if they fall off your head, they are gone. She continued to explain that they have teams that come in and clean the cave three times a day. They only clean the walkway area not the cave itself; they have another team that will do that later.

After about ten minutes, she opened the second door, which entered into another room. Everyone moved to the next room, and they closed that door behind them. This happened three times, each room seamed to get warmer and warmer. As they came into the cave, they understood what the Ranger was talking about. Aggie and Frank were glad they had taken off their coats. Aggie couldn't help think their RV wasn't this warm ever!

According to the Ranger this cavern was inside the mountain, not underneath it. It is a limestone cave and it had "World class features." Aggie and Frank had been in similar types of caverns, but this was unique, it was inside a mountain instead of underground. All the ones they have been in have all been underground.

As they walked along the passage, there was a wide array of unique minerals and formations. There was water percolating from the surface causing calcite formations to continue to grow. It included stalactites dripping down like icicles and giant stalagmites rising up from the ground.

Everything they needed to protect the cavern was built inside the passage ways. The passages were lighted and had cleaning systems that were built into the wall, to protect the cavern. They had talked to other cavern owners and asked them what they did right and what they did wrong to protect their caves. The doors, the lighting, and the cleaning systems are what the research came up with, it worked great!

They followed the Ranger around the passages; a few of the passages were circles, which went through a rock formation. Every turn was incredible, there were mineral formations that looked like soda straws dangling from the ceiling, bacon slabs (of course, this isn't the real name) it just looked like large side of bacon, "really large!"

After about an hour they arrived back in the hallways where they had started from. Before they opened the last door, everyone put back on their coats and got ready to face the cold again. Not only was it around 40 degrees outside, it was sunny. Sun glasses on and gloves! Only in Arizona!

They loaded back on to the train and went back to the visitor center/museum, another adventure done. Next stop food, all that walking made them even hungrier than before. They both were glad it was only fifteen minutes back to the RV.

As they pulled up to the RV, the girls started barking, Frank looked at Aggie and said, "Walk the girls first?" Aggie smiled and said, "Of course!" After their walk, Frank asked Aggie, "Do you what to go to Tombstone tomorrow?" Sounds like a plan, tomorrow we are off to Tombstone!

The next morning they took the girls for a long walk, and then headed off to Tombstone, they would only be gone for a couple hours. Tombstone was 30 miles away, just a hop, skips and jumps away. Aggie found the brochure for the town, which had a little history about the town.

History time: According to the brochure "Tombstone is the most famous of Arizona mining camps with its colorful history. The post office was established in 1878 and it's the same now." Fires nearly caused the death of the town twice. Of Course there is the O.K. Corral shooting with the Earps and Boot Hill. Tombstone is known as "The town too Tough to Die."

They had parked at the far end of town where it wasn't as busy, and walked to the board walk. There weren't that many people around; well it was 9:00 a.m. on Wednesday. Go figure, that's the nice thing about being retired. The real town is a small town, but the streets that are for the tourists were a real live western town at one time. It is about a half mile long and three blocks wide. As they walked down the board walk, there were people dressed like the Wild West, the works "guns, hats and boots."

This time Frank and Aggie planned on eating before they checked out the town. Of course, the only place open was at the other end of the town, all the other places were saloons and didn't serve food until noon.

They stopped and checked out some of the tourist shops, and found a place where they could shoot real old west pistols. Aggie wanted to give it a try, so they went in. They each received six paint ball shots, and a pistol. They both hit the target every time. Aggie even hit the same spot twice, right in the head. Not bad for an old lady, she thought to herself. Frank shot the target around the head every time. He has always been a crack shot, he hasn't shot a gun for at least ten years, but he still has it!

They we're both getting pretty hungry, it was time to fill their guts. So they made a straight shot to the restaurant. They went into the first place they saw that was open. It was a bar, it was called the Oriental.

Aggie asked the bartender if they served food, and he told them no. But they had a menu that belongs to the restaurant across the street. They could order from there, and they would call the order over to the restaurant across the street and they would bring it over to them. It was an interesting concept, but they decided to just go across the street and eat there. The place that they were at smelled like a bar, the smell of cigarette smoke and beer just didn't go well with breakfast. This makes the decision to go across the street easy.

As they headed across the street, an old stage coach went by; Aggie couldn't help notice how big the four horses were! They continued to the restaurant across the street. Frank told Aggie, "It's not that often you have to wait for a stage coach these days!"

When you first go into the restaurant, it looked like a nice size place. But the restaurant was a lot smaller than they first thought. It had a large mirror on the back wall. "Sneaky!" The food was great, they even served Buffalo burgers, but they just had breakfast and headed to their next stop, the O.K. Corral. You can't come to Tombstone and not see a gun fight or the O.K. Corral!

As they waited for the gunfight to start, the wind started picking up and they had sat on the top part of the metal bleachers. Big mistake, they were not protected from the wind; Aggie wished she had a coat. But she had purchased a sweat shirt for Frank Jr., so she put that on. It made it much easier to sit there.

After waiting 20 minutes for the show to start, it wasn't that great. It was ok; Aggie wished it would have been in a larger area, the gunfight now days are done on a side street sound stage. The actors really didn't have the space to shoot each other. She liked the shootouts they use to have on the dirt streets out front. After the show they wandered around and checked out the museums and purchased something for each of the grandkids.

There were all kinds of western souvenir shops in town. Aggie was pretty such, that she could find anything she wanted that pertained to western items there. You can't go to a western town without going to a saloon, it just isn't right if you don't.

They picked, "Big Nose Katie's Saloon, and it was packed. Frank and Aggie found a couple of seats at the bar. They ordered a couple of beers, and when the beer mug was given to them, on one side of the beer mug it said, "Big Nose Katie Saloon, with a picture of her, and on the other side it said, "Big Ass Beer" and they were right!

There was live music in the saloon, the singer was pretty good, and he sang old and new country songs. As Frank and Aggie looked around the bar, at one end there were some old gentlemen and one lady having a great time. By the way they were dressed; Aggie figured they had to be locals. Across the room there was a family dressing up in western clothing and getting their picture taken. At another table there were some people from Switzerland, they had met them earlier, at the O.K Corral. As Frank and Aggie drank their beer, they enjoyed the different shows. It's always fun to people watch, it is great entertainment, and it's free!

It was time to head home, it took an hour and half before they finished drinking their beer, it took awhile, but they did it! They were glad they had something to eat earlier. They also had some distance to walk to the Jeep. It was a short drive to the RV, and as usual the girls were happy to see them and were ready to go for a walk.

The RV Park had filled up while they were gone; they now had company next door, so much for watching the sunrise! The RV that parked next to them was huge and pretty much blocked their view of everything. It's Frank turn to cook dinner, he decided to Bar-B-Q steaks outside. Aggie could eat steak everyday of the week and twice on Sunday. Aggie had marinated the steaks all day in Italian dressing, they always come out great, nice and tender! Another day is gone, who knows what tomorrow may bring.

Today's plan is to go to the tourist information center in Benson. They wanted to see what else there might be to do around the area. The tourist center was located at the old train station; it had a little museum there. As they walked around the center, they found a brochure about the different things they could do around town. The one that looked interesting was Gammons Gulch Movie Set; but they would have to make an appointment.

They decided to just go on a road trip, point the car in a direction and see where they ended up. It's the best way to find things! As they drove down the road, they went through one little town, that had fallen on hard times. The people that were left liked to collect things, some people may call it junk, and others may call it treasure. Either way Frank and Aggie were glad they didn't own the property. They continued to follow the road, when Aggie spotted a sign that said, "Gammons Gulch" Aggie pulled the car off the road and asked Frank should we check it out? Frank reminded Aggie that they had been told they needed to make appointment. Aggie replied, "The worst that can happen is they tell us to go away." They both agreed, what the heck, let's go see!

They drove down a one lane dirt road, they were both glad they had the Jeep, it wasn't the best road. As they pulled up to the gate it was open and a sign that was posted "Open." They drove into the town, and parked the car. As they got out they were not very sure if it was ok or not, there was no one else around. But they figured they are here, why not check it out.

It was a little eerie; there was this western town, out in the middle of nowhere, and no one else around. As they walked towards the first building they noticed the lock was off the door. It looked like something out of the Twilight zone. They still were not sure if they should go inside the building or not. They looked into the windows and it was filled with all kinds of antiques.

They were headed down the steps when they heard a voice and looked up to see an older gentleman in blue overalls and a blue shirt with a baseball hat on. He was all smiles and said, "I didn't see you come in, welcome!" He introduced himself as Jay, and said, "This is my old West town, "Gammons Gulch." He explained that he started building the town in the 1970s, and has been working on it ever since.

As they walked through the town going from building to building Jay entertained them with his stories, about how his father used to work for John Wayne. The town has been used as a movie set for a various movies over the past several years. As they entered the general store he pointed out some different things in there and he said that there were over 500 items in just the general store.

He told a story about a couple that had some energetic children and they were causing some chaos. He said the parents were not paying much attention to their kids.

Somehow or another the kids got into a jar of ginger snaps, which had been in the jar for 20 years. He's pretty sure the kids got sick somewhere along the line!

Then another story he told them was about when he walked into the blacksmith's shop. He opened the door and lying in the middle of the floor was three rattlesnakes. As he quickly started to back up, he told the people that were behind him to back up too, and shut the door. He asked the tourists to stay outside while he took care of business. He went back in and they heard gun fire, three shots. He came back out and told them he took care of the rattlesnakes. He always had his pistol with him; he carried it in his back pocket. He said, "Now before he enters a building he looks through the windows to make sure it's safe to go in.

There was so much to see, he even had his own gallows, church, and many other buildings. He explained that when the movie people wanted to do a movie; if they needed a building they would build it and then leave it there in his town. The saloon was one of these buildings that they had built and left behind. If they didn't want a building in a certain spot they would move it to where they wanted it.

Out of all the Western towns Frank and Aggie had visited, they enjoyed this one the most, it was the best. It took them a couple of hours to walk around the town. It was great listening to Jay's jokes and stories. He would explain how he would find a building in different towns that were dying and bring the building back to his town. The town even had a couple coffins, which Aggie had to get a picture in. Right next to the coffin, there was a sign that read, "Flour Bag 10 cents." Aggie guessed the general store would sell everything.

At the end of the tour, they ended up at the Saloon, where Jay played the piano and told them more stories about the people he had met in the movie industry, and who was nice and who were jerks. Then he played his banjo and told us if we wanted to walk around the town more we were welcome to freely do so.

It was getting late, they decided to head back to the RV and have dinner. It was moving day tomorrow; they will be heading to Deming, New Mexico. After three months of being in Arizona, it was time to head toward Texas.

The kids called later that night and asked how much longer they were going to be on the road. All they could tell them was they would be in El Paso, Texas next week, after that who knows. Twila told them, "Maybe we will meet you at Medina Lake." Aggie told her that would be nice, just let us know.

They had been in Benson for a month; it was time to leave they were getting restless, and was looking forward to be in New Mexico. Benson had been a great central place to see a lot of the southern Arizona.

They loaded the car the day before as usual, and would finish breaking down and putting everything up the next morning, the day of the move. Every time they started loading up the Jeep the night before, Susi would jump into the Jeep and wouldn't get out. You could tell what she was thinking, "You're not leaving me behind!" They decided they would let her stay in the Jeep until they were done.

Frank and Aggie woke up around 5 AM, but it was way too cold and early to break down outside. Aggie made ham and eggs for breakfast, and cleaned up the dishes. While Frank watched his shows, until eight and then it was time for him to get to work.

Aggie secured everything inside and as usual Frank went outside to start disconnecting everything; the electricity, water and sewage. The water line was still frozen; it took a little bit of work to get the hose put back into the RV. Aggie was trying to figure out how many moves they have done. It took a little bit but she figured it was 13 times. No wonder they are getting pretty good at their routine.

Aggie finished everything inside, she double checked to make sure all the cabinets and doors were secure. There is nothing worse than having things flying around as you're driving down the road. Normally, what happens is before they even leave the campground, anything that was loose or unsecured will have flown across the RV or dropped to the floor.

Aggie went outside to see if Frank needed any help. As she rounded the corner there was Frank fighting with the water frozen hose, it looked like he was fighting a snake, and the sewage line was still on the ground.

Frank looked up at Aggie, with a look of disgust and said, "Everything is still frozen!" Aggie replied, "It makes since, it was in the low 20s last night. I guess we have learned another lesson, disconnect waterlines the night before we move, if it's going to freeze." But it looked like Frank was winning the fight with the water hose.

Every move it seems they learn another thing to do. They finally got everything stowed and were on the road by 9:30 AM. Next campsite is in Deming, New Mexico. All they had to do is get on I10 and follow it East to Deming.

The scenery was flat and desolate, the sagebrush and other small bushes were all that you could see for miles. As they climbed up the mountain range into Texas Canyon, the rocks seemed to take on a new life. They were stacked like different animals; Aggie spotted an elephant, turtles, and several other creatures as they drove through the canyon.

Chapter 11

Made it to New Mexico

As they continued down the road, Aggie was following behind Penelope, in the Jeep as usual. But she noticed that Penelope was swaying from side to side. Aggie called Frank on the radio and asked him if everything was okay. He told her "No, he thinks the tires may be low." Every time a truck would go by Penelope, she would sway back and forth. A few times it looked like Frank might go off the road, but he would straighten her back up. It was very nerve-racking for Aggie as she watched Penelope going down the road. Aggie could only imagine how Frank was feeling.

But after thirty miles or so it seemed, once the tires warmed up Penelope appeared to be riding fine. Penelope had been sitting for a month; Aggie guessed it was like putting square tires on the road. Well except for the wind, it would pick up and push Penelope around. Aggie was just glad Frank was driving Penelope instead of her.

Aggie was getting anxious to get back to Texas, but they wanted to spend some time in Deming. They always drove through Deming, New Mexico, when they were stationed at Fort Bliss, TX. They use to take the kids to the "City of the Rocks State Park" Another time Aggie and her parents stopped at the campground there. It was a pretty nice place, and it had all kinds of exotic stones outside they had collected, and it was clean. That is where they planned on spending a couple of days and check out the town.

Three hours later they arrived at their destination in Deming, New Mexico, 91 Palms RV camp grounds. When they checked into the office, they were told they were having a special, "Stay for three days for $60." The plan was to stay for two days, but Aggie said, what the heck, why not!

On the first day, their plan was to set up everything, and then they would take a drive through Deming. They just wanted to see what was in town; they also wanted to find the visitor center. They wanted to get more information about the town. They couldn't find the tourist center, but they figured they would try again tomorrow.

After they drove around for awhile and then went back to camp and just hung around the campground. There was a great place to walk the girls at the campground; it was a dirt road that ran two miles around the campground. Hopefully, they wouldn't have to be pulling out stickers from the girls paws. The other nice thing was the whole campground was fenced in, so they didn't have to worry about wildlife coming in and attacking the dogs. It hasn't happened to them; but they had been warned many times at other campgrounds. They never let the girls out until they checked the area around the RV first.

The campground was the best one yet! It had a nice flat gravel area to park on, and lots of space. The campground wasn't very full yet, but it was still early in the day. Normally, everything starts filling up after 3 p.m. Each campground gets nicer than the last one. Well one exception Wanda's place, was the best!

It was surprising how much there is to do every place that they have stopped at so far. Deming was no different, rocks and minerals are the big thing here. The front office had all kinds of minerals and rocks on display, and some for sale. It took everything Aggie had not to buy any of the stones. But it is still early; they had two more days to go in Deming. The campground was called 81 Palms; of course Aggie had to start counting all the palm trees. After finding 65 she gave up, they were all around the campground, some big ones and lots of little ones.

The next morning it was cold, it was in the low 30s, by 9am it was in the 40s, so they figured they would go to the museum first. The lady in the office had told them about it earlier. She told them that it was huge and lots of different items in it.

They headed over to take a shower before leaving. As they were walking over to the shower room they noticed the RV next to them had solid ice all down the side of it. It looked like the water had come out from a broken waterline during the night. It was pretty, but Frank and Aggie laughed and Frank said, "Someone is not going to be too happy!" Aggie just smiled and agreed. When they came back from the shower, the ice was all knocked off the rig and lying on the ground. Aggie wanted to take a picture of the huge ice icicle, but oh well guess not!

The museum is called "Deming Luna Mimbers Museum." The city of Deming was founded in 1881; it was an important port of entry on the US-Mexican border until the Gadsden Purchase of 1853. It had a nickname at one time, "New Chicago." Because of the surge of railroad usage, it was expected that it would resemble Chicago, Illinois. "There are numerous ancient Native-American sites around Deming. The Mimbers and Casas Grandes cultures made pottery of remarkable quality, and the Deming area is rich in native pottery artifacts, as well as beads, stone implements, stone carvings, graves, etc," according to the flyer Aggie had picked up.

They arrived at the museum; it was a large old brick building, it was built in the beginning as the National Guard Armory. There was a sign that directed them to the basement door. As they entered the museum, it looked like it wasn't too big; it shouldn't take too long to go through. Boy was they ever wrong!

The lady at the front desk explained a little about the museum, then handed them a map of the museum. She said, "You may need this!" Frank and Aggie looked at each other and then the map. The first room they walked into was the Old Timer's Room; it displayed old photographs of the people in the town and the pictures of the town before and after the fire in 1899.

Each room and floor had something different to look at. They wandered around for a while together, then Frank found the military area and Aggie found the Gem and rock section. During their wanderings they kept running into a gentleman named Bob. He was a talker; he had been in the Navy. Frank and he spent quite a bit of time in the military room. Aggie spent most of her time looking in the gem room.

The museum was an incredible place to visit; you could tell a lot of work was done to make this a unique place to visit. Aggie purchased a book at the gift shop about the "Deming

Luna Mimbers Museum," by Ruth Brown. It took a week before she read it, by then they were already at Ft. Bliss.

She wished she would have read the book before leaving Deming. They had missed so much at the museum, which was outside. After reading the book, she discovered there was so much history in that little town in New Mexico.

After the museum, they stopped and had lunch, and then went back to the RV and picked up the girls. They wanted to go visit the City of the Rocks State Park, it wasn't that far and it was nice and warm out today. This way they could take the girls for a hike too.

City of the Rocks had changed a lot; the state park had added a visitor center/museum, a cactus garden, and a RV camping area. Other than that the rocks pretty much looked the same. The days when they would climb all over the rocks with the kids are gone. They walked around and tried to figure out where they had camped with the kids. Susi loved it; she got on the scent of something and was all over the place.

As they were walking around, Aggie spotted a hawk on a tall stone watching them. Aggie turned to Frank and told him, "I guess he is the guard!" Frank replied, "Just keep an eye on him, he may try to take one of the girls!" Aggie didn't think of that, maybe it's time to go. That's all she needed was for a hawk to pick up one of the girls. She could see Frank and her running through the desert, throwing rocks and screaming at the hawk. What a site that would have been!

On the way out they stopped at the visitor center, as they were walking into the center, they ran into Bob and his wife. Frank had told them about the park as they talked at the Deming museum. It was like running into old friends, Bob told them that Frank had made it sound so interesting they had to come and see what he was talking about. They were heading into the park, Frank told them enjoy and they headed into the center. The little museum at the center had displays of the different animals and plants from the area. There was a painting on the wall, and they asked you to find all 35 of the animals in the picture. Between the two of them, they finally found all of the animals. They didn't even cheat; there was a map at the bottom where it showed where all of the animals were. As they left the center, they wanted to check out the new campground. It was pretty nice; every state park they had been though has been nice. They normally weren't very full. Aggie told Frank; maybe we should stay at a few of them sometime.

Chapter 12

Back in Texas

It was time to move to their next stop, Ft. Bliss, TX. They have friends that still lived there. It was a short drive, 125 miles, they were there by noon, and were sitting outside enjoying the sun by 2:00. Frank told Aggie, this is pretty sweet weather for February. They really didn't have too many plans, just to visit Judy and check out their old house. As normal, Frank wanted to check out the Post. The Post RV Park had doubled in size, since the last time they were there.

They called their friend Judy, to let her know they had arrived. They agreed to meet the next evening at her house. In the morning they went for a ride, they couldn't believe how big El Paso had grown. Their house was on the edge of the desert when they lived there, and now the town goes ten miles passed their old house. There are two large malls, just down the street from their old house. Aggie told Frank, if they had all these businesses when they lived there, she wouldn't have wanted to move.

The weather was wonderful; it was in the forties in the morning, and in the 70s during the day. Their plan was to hang out in Ft. Bliss for a week. They had taken a back road into town, so Aggie wanted to check out the visitor center on I10, on the other side of the mountain. The Franklin Mountains runs north to south splitting El Paso. Trans Mountain road had not changed much, there were pull offs so you could check out the view. Twenty five years ago the pull offs were there, just not as nice, they have restrooms now. At that time you could see the edge of the city, but now there is no end to it. Amazing how fast a town can grow in a short amount of time.

As they came down the pass on the west side, they could see I10 and it was all backed up on the east bound lanes. They were glad they were going west back to New Mexico. Since they were going east, they saw the problem, bad accident. Frank told Aggie, "I bet it will be on the news tonight," Aggie agreed with him.

They found the New Mexico Information Center, and it was nice, it is the oldest Information Center on I10, which says a lot. In its hay day it looked like it was a great place to stop. Now it's just a small room, with the information about the area. Next stop was the Texas Information Center (IC); the problem was that it was east bound, where the accident was. The traffic was backed up all the way to the exit they were on. One nice thing about freeways they usually have a side road that runs along the side. It was going pretty good, until they got closer to the accident, people were driving across the divider. They were glad the IC wasn't that far down the road.

The Texas IC was huge; it had all the information broken down by the different areas of Texas. It even had a place that you could take a picture with a back ground of the Texas flag; there were even cowboy hats they could put on. Aggie came out of the center, with two handfuls of brochures and maps from the different areas of Texas.

They were hoping that the traffic would have been cleared off before they headed back that way, but no such luck. It was even worse than before. The drive that should have taken ten minutes ended up taking 40 minutes. They were supposed to have lunch with Judy, so they had to call her and push out lunch. They ended up having to go the long way back to camp.

After meeting Judy for lunch they went back to camp and took the girls out for their walk around the campground. It was a beautiful day, and the evening was nice and warm, so they went out for another walk without the girls.

The rest of the week went pretty quick, they would run around and check out Ft. Bliss and the places they used to hang out when they lived here. It's true you can't go home, everything had changed so much. Ft. Bliss had tripled in size and El Paso only had one freeway when they lived there before, now there are three or four freeways. Aggie lost count! They would enjoy the company of Judy, in the evening. Judy lived in a beautiful home about half way up the mountain; it overlooked Ft. Bliss and some of El Paso from her backyard. Frank and Aggie were glad they could spend some time with her, and meet her son and grandson. She was one busy women, and so full of energy and life! The week visit at the Fort Bliss Army Travel Camp went by all too fast, Frank thought. On Monday they will be leaving and heading on into Texas.

Their next stop was Ft. Stockton, TX and then on to Lake Hills, TX for three weeks. It was a quick trip to Ft. Stockton from Ft. Bliss; they were only going to be in Ft. Stockton for three days. Ft. Stockton looked to be an interesting place; it has a lot a history around it.

The RV Park they stayed at was nice, it uses to be a KOA and then it changed to Good Sam. They could see the KOA sign on the roof of the "A" Frame Office building and in the shower the tiles had K O A. The people that ran it were very nice; it was of course by the freeway. All Aggie could think of was the movie; Planes, Trains and Automobiles, everywhere they have stayed they could always hear one of them!

Aggie had a brochure about Ft. Stockton, of course! They planned on checking the Old Fort out tomorrow. It was originally called Camp Stockton in 1858; in 1870's it became Fort Stockton. According to the brochure, it consists of the original and reconstructed military buildings.

History time! The first troops to arrive at Camp Stockton were the 1st and 8th Infantry U.S. Army. The soldier's job was to protect travelers and settlers that came on the numerous roads and trails leading to this area. Because there was abundance of water, that supplied Comanche Springs. It was here that the trails crossed and received the name "Comanche War Trail." Camp Stockton was abandoned when the Civil War began."

In July 1867 the fort came alive again, when the 9th Cavalry and the "Buffalo Soldiers," which was composed of black enlisted men arrived. The Fort was abandoned in 1886, as the frontier moved west. The post-war fort was occupied for nineteen years (1867-1886)."

As usual the next morning, they had to drive around the town and check it out. It was a nice, clean town. They arrived at the Fort around 10:00 a.m. and found a place to park. There was only one other car, but they didn't see anyone around. There was a sign showing what the Fort use to look like and showed the building numbers, but didn't say what they were. It was weird but oh well, as they walked to the first building they could tell it had to be the jail, or what the military called the "Stockade."

As they entered the building which was made up of bricks and mud, there was a sign that explained it was "The Guardhouse," it was one of the first buildings completed, it contained a jailer's quarters, three solitary confinement cells and a large holding cell." It was warm outside but inside the building it was cold, and the cells only had one little window at top. The three solitary confinements cells there had no light and they still had the leg iron chained to the wall, they must have used. Aggie told Frank, just seeing this room would have kept me from doing anything wrong. Frank laughed and agreed, "It would have sucked to be in here!"

They continued to walk around the Fort, when they found the visitor center/museum, it was on the other side from where they had parked the car earlier. The lady at the front desk welcomed them and explained what was in the Fort and museum, which was located in the same building as the visitor center. She said, "There are six buildings that are part of the fort; the jail, three Officer's Quarters, OQ #7, and a Barracks which is the Visitor center."

The receptionist was a Native American; she has lived here her whole life in Fort Stockton. Even her ancestors all lived in the area. She was half Apache and half Comanche. She told them about the stories that she heard in her childhood. Her grandmother use to tell her stories to keep her in line.

After they finished looking at the items in the museum they walked around the Fort. The enlisted barracks was set up the way it would have been back in the 1800's; it was remarkable how they use to live. It had to get really cold in the winter, the walls were thin, and there was no sign of a fireplace. There were beds that had iron head and foot ends, and half inch boards going the length of the bed, they would adjust the boards for the length of the soldier, then they had a one inch mattress with a wool blanket, and at the end of their bed was a foot locker.

The Officers buildings were under reconstruction, but they looked in the windows, and they could tell it was much nicer then the enlisted quarters. Everything was set up pretty much the same as the other Camp/Forts they have visited in the last few months. After checking out the rest of the Fort, they drove around town, it was a nice place and they discovered there is lots more to see in the area. Aggie suggested to Frank, maybe they could stop longer if they came back this way again. Frank agreed and said, "By the looks of it there is a lot of history in this area, the brochure we picked up at the center, shows there is five other camps that use to be part of the Comanche trails."

They were getting hungry so they headed back to camp; Frank was going to BBQ some chicken tonight.

CHAPTER 13

Heading to the Texas
Hill country

Today is another day of travel; their next stop is Sonora, TX. According to the GPS, Sonora, TX is only 145 miles away; it shouldn't take long to get to the next campground. They will be staying at Sonora Caverns for three nights and then moving on to Medina Lake Campground in Lake Hills, TX for three weeks.

It didn't take long to break down this time; they didn't unload the Jeep and just moved the boxes from the bedroom to the dash inside the RV. The boxes would be out of the way for the two nights. The only things that they unpacked were the coffee pot, and night items. In the morning they would be leaving so they would move the boxes back to the bedroom and disconnected the power and water and be off. It took less than thirty minutes, and they were on the road again. Their plan was to do the same process when they stayed at Sonora Cavern RV Park.

When they left Ft. Stockton, the weather was nice for a change, it wasn't windy or rainy. Earlier that morning it was blowing pretty hard around 6:00 a.m. but by 8:30 a.m. it had died down, so they headed out. Aggie took the lead; it was a nice change for her, they arrived at Sonora with no problems, two and half hours later. It was nice not having to look at the back of the RV, for a change. She actually was able to look at the scenery in front of her for the next fourteen miles, instead of looking at the back of Penelope.

Once they were on the freeway, Frank would always take the lead, mostly because Aggie had the tendency of leaving him behind. She knew when she had gone too far, because she couldn't reach Frank on the radio. The hard part for Aggie was when she was in front of Frank; she tried not to get too far ahead of him. So she would take the lead going in and out of the campground, just in case there was any surprises, Aggie could warn Frank. Then she would let Frank take the lead on the highway.

They had forgotten how far off the road Sonora Cavern campground was, it was a good eight miles from the main highway. But the best thing about it was, they were far from the freeway, no cars or train sounds for a change. When they arrived there was only two rigs, but by six, it was full.

By noon the next day, they were the only ones left; everyone else had left first thing in the morning. So they had the whole place to themselves, well except for the people that worked at the campground. It was so quite there, as they walked around the park they had found a large stone that had some kind of fossil in it. It looked like a husk of some kind.

The rock was too big to pick up. Frank thought to himself, thank goodness!

The last time they were there, it was during the summer. The place was pretty full; it was filled with a lot of families. Their kids and grandkids were with them on the last visit, everyone had a great time. This time they enjoyed the quiet and the time to themselves. There was a lot of deer the last time they were here. This time they didn't see any wild life.

Around three p.m., everyone started coming in, before six the lower parking area was filled. There were still lots of space at the upper level. Frank had parked in the lower area. The only space left in the lower area was next to them and it was a pretty small area, so they figured no one would park there.

To their surprise around 9:00 p.m., a large Class A, RV came in from the wrong direction and pulling a car. As they watched from their window, they saw it come about two feet away from the end of their rig. Frank decided he better go check out what was going on out there. Because they had knocked the TV off the air, his RV was blocking the satellite signal. Frank wanted to make sure they didn't hit anything. When he went out there, the old guy was trying to unhook his car.

As Frank came out of the RV, the man smiled at Frank and said, "Did I knock you off the air?" As Aggie was watching out the window, she saw Frank talking to the guy. The next thing you know Frank is helping him disconnect his car from their RV. Frank held the flashlight, while the guy disconnected it. After they were done Frank handed him back the flashlight, and went back into Penelope.

They ended up parking their RV at an angle to fit into the small space and parked the car in the parking space across the way. The guy in the RV told Frank, they were planning on moving tomorrow when it was daylight out. But tonight they plan on just spending the night where they were. It would be much easier to find a place tomorrow in the daylight, after everyone had left. Frank and Aggie planned on leaving first thing in the morning, so they didn't worry about them.

As they were heading down the country road she was driving slowly. Aggie looked to the right and there were two small deer looking at her. As she continued to drive down the road she looked off to the left of the road and there were four more deer just standing in the field, looking at her. It was as if they were letting her know that they were there and saying goodbye. She had to radio Frank and let him know that she finally had spotted some deer. Frank acknowledged that he did see them.

The first 40 miles they had nice weather and there was no wind and very little traffic, it was a nice change. Then the nightmare started, first the wind started blowing Penelope all over the road. Aggie even had to keep both of her hands on the steering wheel, just to keep the Jeep on the road.

She could only imagine what Frank was doing to keep Penelope on the road. The nightmare continued the traffic caught up with them. The big rigs were flying by them at 75 mph, and the wind was pushing Penelope from the right. As Penelope swayed from right to left, Frank kept her between the lines. Aggie couldn't help but think, "What a man!"

Finally, the wind let up! It was nice that they didn't have to fight to keep the rigs on the road. As they were coming off of the mountain Aggie spotted a sign that said, "Beware of high winds." All Aggie could think was, it's a little late for that warning. They have been fighting the winds for the last fifteen miles.

As they were driving down the freeway Aggie took notice of the weird things that were coming down the road on the other side of the freeway. Most of the rigs had normal things they usually pulled, box car, trailers, and cars. But there were a few things that had caught her eye. For example there was this thing that had to be as long as a large airplane wing, she thought it was lying on its side. It was fourteen feet wide on one end and then it narrowed down to a fine point. It was lying on two trailer beds and it was white. Aggie called Frank and asked if he had seen it, he said no, he was too busy watching the road in front of him. Aggie couldn't understand how he could have missed it, but on the other hand, it really wasn't a surprise. Oh Well, that was Frank when he drove he watched the road in front of him, he even watched the road when Aggie was driving. Aggie didn't mind that, that way she could look around, while she was driving.

Aggie took after her dad, her dad was a wonderful driver, and he could drive and still enjoy the scenery around him. Aggie was the same way, which drove Frank crazy. Frank and Aggie would be driving along, and if Aggie saw a cool house or something unusual on the side of the road, she would say something to Frank about it. He would say he didn't see it, because he was watching the road, and he was the passenger.

The next 70 miles was nice, light traffic and good weather. Then the problems started! The exit they took went right into the middle of a big town with heavy traffic. According to the directions they had gotten from the GPS, they only had to go a half mile down the road. Which Aggie really didn't think it was going to be a big deal, because it was only for a short distance. When they arrived at where they were supposed to turn, there was no road, it was now a mall. They had no choice, but to continue on down the road, there was no place to turn off or even space to turnaround.

It's not that easy to stop an RV on a dime. By now Aggie had taken the lead. She was going to find a road that they needed to turn on or someplace to pull off the road. But after driving another three miles, the road they were suppose to turn on wasn't there. She started looking for a place to pull off and regroup.

As she came over the hill, she saw a gas station, she radioed Frank about it, but it was too late, he was almost at the top of the hill. Frank couldn't pull over in time; he ended up pulling off farther down on the side of the road. The funny part was the car that was behind him followed him and parked behind him. The driver must of figured out he had pulled off the road instead of stopping on the road, she looked a little upset and then she went around him.

Aggie radioed Frank and told him to go on down the road, and stop somewhere, where he could pull off the road completely. Finally, they found a place that they could both pull off and look at the map. Neither one of them were too happy at this point. There was a turn off on the right side of the road; she radioed Frank to let him know, hopefully this time it would give him enough warming. It was, Frank pulled over and opened the door and the girls came jumping out of the RV, and they must really need to get out she guessed. While Frank was herding the girls back into the RV, Aggie had put the address to the RV campground into her phone, to figure out where they were.

According to the GPS, it looked like they had another 40 miles to go. She showed the directions to Frank, and they figured out they had to turn around and go back about a mile. Using the GPS on Aggies phone, it told her to go 18 miles down this road and then turn left and go another 9 miles and turn right and go another nine miles and so on. Frank was getting tired; they had been on the road for four hours, and it was only supposed to take two and one half hours. What a nightmare!

CHAPTER 14

Medina Lake Campground

Finally after five hours they found the campground, it was only suppose to be 156 miles, they ended up driving 190 miles. They were now in the Texas Hill Country! It didn't take long to check in, and that was a good thing, they were both pretty tired and hungry. Aggie hadn't eaten all day and needed to use the restroom.

The campground was huge, it was called Medina Lake Campground, after driving around a little bit; they finally found a spot to park. There were lots of space in between the RV's, and lots of trees. It may be February but it was going to be in the 80's this week.

They got Penelope set up and took the girls out to do their business. Aggie made some sandwiches for dinner; she wasn't in the mood to cook. It had been a long stressful day; she was looking forward to hitting the sack. But they still had to take the girls out for their walk. So after everything was settled in, they headed out for their walk. It was an amazing place; they could see the lake from where they had set up camp.

It was so quiet there; there was no freeway, trains or airplanes to hear. The only sounds that they heard were the birds singing. There were so many types of birds there; they even saw a few squirrels on their walk.

It was a nice evening, they decided to sit outside and enjoy it while they could. The air was fresh and clean, and no neighbors around. So far anyway! After a little while the deer started showing up, first there was a little doe and her baby, and then more does and their babies started showing up. Aggie had noticed earlier a guy was throwing something on the ground; it looks like corn to her. First thing that came to her mind; they were feeding the birds and squirrels. But now she knew why. As they watched more and more deer came, some would leave and others would take their place. You could tell this wasn't the first time they had been feed by this guy. By the time they all had gathered around there must have been thirty deer. They were smaller than the ones that they had seen in Oregon.

It was also weird how they stayed in a herd. Normally, deer don't travel in herds, they are more loners. These deer were not afraid of humans, a few were a little skittish, but the corn kept them there.

After about an hour they started moving off into the woods across the street from them. The woods weren't that thick, but the deer would disappear in a matter of seconds.

Aggie couldn't help thinking what a great way to end the day! They needed to move everything undercover. They had heard earlier in the weather forecast, a storm was coming in. It was going to be heavy rain and wind, most of the night.

Frank told Aggie, "It took the rain a little while to find us this time!" Yea, but you know Texas rain storms, it's either one that will wash you away, or barely wash your car! They finally put everything undercover and went into the RV.

Just as they were settling in for the evening, their daughter Maria called. The first thing she asked was, "Where are you now?" Aggie had to laugh, every time one of the kids called, that's the first thing they asked. Aggie told her we're outside of San Antonio, in Lakehills; it's on Medina Lake. Maria replied, "That's not too far from Houston, how long are you going to be there? Frank told her, just a couple of weeks, it's really nice here. Are you coming home after Lakehills? Maria asked. Aggie told her, "No we're going to Columbus after this." Maria replied, "We were all talking about coming and visiting you guys this coming weekend." Both Frank and Aggie, replied at the same time, Great! Maria told them they would be there Friday night. Aggie told her that would be wonderful, why don't you bring the party boat with you? The lake is pretty big and beautiful. Maria told her, that was the plan. I'll let the rest of the kids know, and we'll see you this weekend. Love you! Aggie replied back, Love ya too, and we're looking forward to seeing everyone. They said their good-byes and hung up the phone.

Frank smiled at Aggie; it'll be great to see the family! Aggie was still smiling she was excited about seeing everyone. The rest of the evening they talked about what they could do while the kids were there.

The next morning they took the girls out for their morning walk. They figured that they would explore the area down by the lake. It was a beautiful blue; there was a little island in the middle of the lake. As they walked along the lake edge, Aggie spotted some seashells, which they thought was a little weird since it wasn't the ocean.

As they continued walking along the shoreline they came to an area where they couldn't walk by the water edge. They had to go in land to go around the area. As they walked in land they discovered a lot more shells and driftwood, it felt like they were on a beach. It was a good 100 feet from the water's edge. Frank and Aggie figured the water had to be a good 15 feet deeper at one time, for all the shells and driftwood that was lying out in the field. They had heard from the neighbor, that the lake had been empty for the last few years.

As they continued their walk, they would meet other campers; the full time people were always friendly. But the weekend campers pretty much kept to themselves. They stopped and visited with a lady that was spreading corn in the field next to her rig. The lady said that she usually goes through about 200 pounds of corn, while she's there. She feeds the deer every day and some will eat out of her hands. She has been coming here every year for the last ten years. She continued to tell them, this is the first time the lake has been full in the last three years. It was just a little creek at the bottom of the lake and people would drive their ATVs in it. They would drive up and down the lake walls, and cross into the campground. The Ranger told them that, they had a lot of break-ins while the water was down.

They heard earlier from a guy, that a farmer even put a fence in the middle of the lake, which was his property. He would let the cattle graze down in the lake bottom. With the lake full, Aggie could just imagine having a scuba diver down there and run into wire fencing.

They continued to see deer everywhere they walked, first there was five in one place and then ten, and then a little ways down the road there would be another ten or so. The deer weren't even scared of them; they would just look up at them and go back to eating. As they were walking along they saw this old buck, it was darker than the rest. He must have been the oldest one in the herd. He had long curved hoofs that were split, and had a ragged hide. He looked horrible but he just walked on by them. He went into the field with the rest of them and waited for the new younger buck of the herd to let him into the field. It was sad to watch, but at least he was still alive and must have had a long life.

Their kids will be there in three days, they wanted to check out the towns around them, to see if there was anything fun to do. The couple next door they had met at the Benson site. Rich and Jennie have been coming to Median Lake for the last five years. They told them about a steakhouse, which had great steaks and live music with a dance floor. Thursday night was ladies night, and you get to pick your own steak night.

The plan was in place, they would go to dinner Thursday night with Jennie and Rich. The kids would be arriving on Friday night. Aggie figured if it was a nice place maybe they could take the kids on Saturday night, for a little dancing. It's been awhile since Frank and Aggie had been out dancing.

The next morning they went for their walk with the girls. The birds were singing and talking to each other. The white tail deer were out eating their breakfast. There was a little breeze, but that changed as they got closer to the lake. They came out of the tree line and as they were getting closer to the lake, the wind started to pick up and was blowing steady. When they arrived at the water's edge, the wind had picked up. It felt like it was blowing about 15 miles an hour. It blew Frank's hat right off his head, so he ended up chasing it down the road. Every time he reached down to pick up his hat, the wind would blow it farther down the road. He finally stepped on it, and picked it up and put it inside his jacket. He told

Aggie, "I'll put it on later." It wasn't too much fun for the girls either; the wind kept pushing them to the side as they walked.

It was time to go back into the tree line; the strong winds were getting too much for them! Frank told Aggie, "Let's just follow the trails inside the campground this morning!" Aggie had to, Agree!

They were both surprised how different the weather was from inside the tree line, where they had set up their camp. It was weird how different the weather was. They were maybe 30 yards inside the tree line, from the lake. They both agreed they had picked a great spot to set up camp. It was far enough away from the weekenders, and the winds of the lake.

That evening they got all fixed up and ready to go dancing and dining with Jennie and Rick. They took the Jeep, because Jennie's and Rick's car was just too small for everyone. As they loaded up, Rick told Jennie, "Look my legs fit inside, and I even have head room! Jennie just smiled and said, "Well enjoy it while you can!" Rick didn't say another word about the car. They had a little Smart car, which was great on gas, but not much space for anything else.

They arrived at the Saloon/Restaurant; Aggie couldn't help but think this place is huge! They walked down the board walk, they entered though two swinging doors, and it looked like an old western hotel. The siding was old gray colored wood. The bar was to the left and the first dining area was to the right. There were two more dining rooms in the back; the hostess led them to the back dining area. It didn't take long to be seated. It was still early, it was 4:00 pm, and the dinner crowd hadn't arrived yet. As they walked through the dining area, Aggie checked out the different meals people were eating. It all looked so good! As they walked into the dining area Aggie could smell the steaks cooking on the grill. Aggie loved that smell, there is nothing like a good grilled steak. It was a great spot to sit; they could see the people around them. The fire pit, which they cooked the steaks on, was right in front of them. Aggie couldn't help thinking what a great place!

The waitress took their drink order and then the cook brought the raw steaks over, so they could pick which one they wanted. There were T-bone, New York, Filet Mignon, and a large Pork steak. Three of them picked T-bone, and Jennie picked the pork steak. The cook asked them a few questions about how they liked their steaks. Then he went over to the grill, and seasoned them and laid the steaks on to the grill and they started sizzling. They could see the smoke going up into the fan. As they watched the steaks cooking, it really started getting busy. It was nice they had the family with kids in one section, and the adults without kids, in the back section. They all loved kids, but sometimes it's just nice to have adults around.

The meal was wonderful, they were all full, and the waitress asked if they wanted dessert, they all said No! She just smiled, and laid the bill on the table, and said she would take it when they were ready. Frank handed her his credit card, and off she went. As they were waiting for her return, they could hear music coming from the outside deck. Aggie couldn't help herself; she told Jennie lets go see what's going on out there. Jennie stood up and started leading the way.

They went through double doors out to the deck; there was a huge dance floor, with a bar and tables to sit at. Jennie turned to Aggie, "Let's go get the guys and do a little dancing." Aggie agreed and headed back to the table with Jennie. The guys had paid the bill and were headed toward the door. Jennie grabbed Rich's arm and Aggie grabbed Frank's arm and told them we're going dancing. They told the guys, as they pulled them onto the dance floor, "No argument." The guys knew better then to argue with them.

After the first dance, they found a table right off of the dance floor. They ordered some drinks and people watched for a little while. It was pretty nice out on the deck. It was warm but a little breeze would come though every so often, it was always at the right time. Aggie hoping she could get one dance out of Frank before he settled into his chair. He wasn't much of a dancer, but to her surprise Frank got up and asked her to dance. It took a couple of seconds to reply, she was surprised that he asked her. Usually, Aggie was the one that asked him; normally she could get him to do a couple of slow dances. The song that was playing was a fast dance, of course she said yes, and jumped up and grabbed him before he changed his mind.

As they got out to the dance floor, Aggie told him, this is a nice surprise. He replied, "It's our song!" Aggie didn't say anything, she had no clue it was their song. Oh well, it got him out on the dance floor.

Jennie looked at Rich, and he knew what that met, so he got up and reached for her hand, and told her, "Come on babe, let's show them how it's done!" Jennie had a big smile on her face as they walked out to the floor. Both couples stayed out on the dance floor for three songs. They were all out of shape, so three songs were pretty good, even the ladies were ready to take a break.

When they got back to their table the waitress was right there, so they ordered another round and sat down to watch the dancers on the floor. As they watched the people on the dance floor, they noticed a woman that looked like she was having a hard time staying on her feet. It looked like she may have had a little too much to drink. The man that she was with wasn't much better off. At first it was funny, there weren't that many people on the dance floor, and they were having fun.

After a little bit they went and sat down. As the evening continued, the floor started to fill up. There were some pretty good dancers out there. They went out a few more times, but it was more fun to watch everyone. The drunken couple came back onto the floor. They both looked like they could fall down at any minute. The woman continued to try to dance and her man just laughed and yelled "Go babe, Go!" She would keep running into one person then another.

Then she ran into the wrong person, it was the guy's x-girlfriend. She turned and saw her x-boyfriend with the drunken woman and told him, "Why don't you take this old drunker home. The drunken woman yelled at her, "Who you calling old?" You bitch! The drunken woman pushed her, and then the pushing started. As Aggie and her group watched, they couldn't help but wonder who was going to take the first swing. The x-boyfriend tried to pull his girlfriend away, when his girlfriend grabbed a handful of hair from his x.

That's when his face turned, you could read it, and it said, "Oh Shit!" That's all it took, the women were into it, everyone backed away, but the band just kept playing. The boyfriend pulled them apart, but the drunken woman wouldn't let it go. The x-girlfriend started to walk away, when the drunken woman came up behind her and yelled, "Where do you think you're going?" The x turned to her and told her to get away from her and pushed her.

By now they were right next to Frank and Aggies table, the drunken lady landed on Riche's lap. The expression on his face was priceless, he was in shock and wasn't sure what he should do. The drunken woman smiled at him and said, "Hi there big fellow!" All Richie could do is smile and look at her huge breasts, which was right in his face.

Needless to say, that this didn't sit well with Jennie, she pushed the woman off his lap. The woman stood up and turned to say something when the Bouncer came up to her. He told her she had to leave, as he grabbed her arm to lead her out. She started yelling at him, and screaming at the x-girlfriend, "This is all ya fault!" The x just laughed at her and walked back to her table.

The drunken boyfriend decided he should do something, to protect his woman. He told the Bouncer to take his damn hands off her. The Bouncers replied you need to go too! The guy took a swing at the Bouncer, who was twice as big as him. He hit the Bouncer in the chest, which just bounced off him. The expression on the guys face was, "Oh shit!" Aggie couldn't help but think, what an idiot!

At that point, two other Bouncers showed up, and the guy figured he was better off taking his woman and leaving. The Bouncers lead them to the front door, where the police were waiting for them. The show was over and it was time for the drunken couple to go.

On the way home, they talked about the evening; it was a great evening, even with the fight. Jennie turned to Richie and said you sure looked like you enjoyed her landing on your lap. "Really, what did you want me to do?" She laughed and said, "Not enjoy it so much, as she hit him in the arm." They all laughed and pulled into the RV Park. They said their good nights, as Frank and Aggie walked up to their RV. They saw a note on their RV door. Aggie read it, it's from Twila, they decided to come down early and they are parked at E10, and come see them when they got back.

Frank knew that look, he told Aggie "No, it's late we'll go see them tomorrow. Aggie smiled and said it wouldn't hurt to go see if they are still up, and it's only 11:00, as she headed toward their camp site. When they turned the corner they could see Twila and Dennis's trailer. There was one light on in the front, they weren't sure if they were up or not. But as they got closer Twila opened the trailer door, and ran toward them. Both Frank and Aggie were surprised that she was so excited to see them.

Then Twila said, "Where have you been? I've been worried sick about you guys. You didn't answer your phone, and no one knew where you were." Finally, she took a breath. Aggie gave her a big hug, and said we're sorry we were at a Saloon with some friends. Why are you here? You guys were supposed to come in tomorrow. Are you the only ones here? Twila explained, "Dennis didn't want to fight the traffic, so he took off early, we thought it would be a nice surprise. Yes, we're the only ones here. I figured this would be the only time we would have you to ourselves. So much for that idea," she said with a frown on her face. Aggie just laughed and said, Poor babe!

About that time Dennis came out of the trailer. First thing he said was, "Well it's about time you came home, and Twila has been driving me nuts. She had you lying in a ditch somewhere or in a hospital. By the way where were you? Don't old people stay home and wait for their children to come visit?" Frank laughed, and told him, "That's what I keep telling her, but she won't listen to me. Where are the granddaughters?" Dennis told him, "Their sleeping, like we should be doing. How about we see you guys in the morning for breakfast?" Mom you get to cook your potatoes surprise. Aggie told him sure thing, I have everything I need to make it, and we'll see you around 7. Dennis told her, "Let's make it 8! Twila looked at him, and said fine 8. Frank told them all, "Eight is better! There were hugs all around and Frank and Aggie went back to their rig.

Both Frank and Aggie slept wonderfully. The only reason they woke up was because the girls were barking and jumping on them. It was 7:00 a.m. and that was when they normally would take the dogs out to do their business.

Aggie patted Frank on the back and told him it's his turn. I need to start getting breakfast ready; the kids are supposed to be here at 8. As Frank got out of bed, Aggie asked him, "How do you feel about cooking the bacon outside? "Sure why not," Frank replied.

The girls were barking ready to go outside, they ran to the door and then back to the bedroom. Aggie said, I think they really had to go! Frank barely got to the door and had it open. They were out looking for a place to go. As Frank stepped out of the RV he heard, "Howdy Neighbor!" It was Twila and the girls, Sharlene and Tina. Frank waved at them, and the girls started running toward him yelling, "Grandpa we missed you!" Frank couldn't help but to smile from ear to ear. He sure missed them.

He gave each of them a big bear hug and a kiss. He told them he missed them too! About that time Aggie came out and asked, "Where are my hugs. Again the girls screamed, this time for Grandma, and bear hugs all around again.

Frank asked Twila, "Where is Dennis?" Twila told him, "Oh he is putting the boat in the water. He wanted to get the boat into the water before it started getting busy, he should be here shortly."

Tina and Sharlene were talking a mile a minute; they had so much to tell their grandparents. It was Grandma this and Grandpa did you know. Poor Twila couldn't get in a word. Then she told them, "Why don't you go see where your Dad is at?" O.K. Mom, and off they went, they took off like they were being chased by something. As they ran off, they yelled, "We'll be right back!" Frank and Aggie waved at them and said we'll be here!

Twila smiled and told them finally I have you to myself. She gave them both big hugs; I sure have missed you guys. Aggie told her we have missed you too, sweetie. So what's been going on in your life, Aggie asked. Oh nothing much, oh yeah, we're going to adopt a little boy. Aggie and Frank were surprised, as Twila got a big smile on her face.

"It is Dennis's nephew, I told you about his mom being very sick and that we have been taking care of him the last few months. Well she passed away two weeks ago. She had asked us to adopt Jesse before she died, so there wouldn't be any problems. He's only 10 and his father left a long time ago. He had a pretty hard life so far." Twila explained.

Where is he now? Frank asked. Twila told him, his coming with Frankie. He really likes to hang out with Daniel and Douglas. Aggie gave her a big hug and said, "That's great that you guys are there for him. I know Dennis has always wanted a boy. Twila replied, "Yea, Jessie thinks Dennis walks on water! He is a great kid, and the girls love him.

Sharlene came running up to Aggie and yelled, "I win!" Aggie told her, I guess you get another hug from me! Tina you'll have to get one from Grandpa you're the loser. Frank said, "Hey!" They all laughed, as Dennis walked up to them and said, "Where's breakfast?"

Aggie and Twila laughed, and Frank walked over with a plate of bacon. "Well here's my part, where is your part Aggie?" It's ready I just need to put cheese on it, Aggie told him. Aggie asked the girls, "Do you want to help me?" They followed Aggie into the RV, Aggie handed them the plate and all the other items needed to have breakfast. They were eating when Aggie got a call from Frankie, telling her they should be there in about an hour. Maria is following behind them. At the end of the conversation he said, "I'm glad you guys are ok,

Twila was pretty worried about you." Aggie told him, Yea, I know I heard all about it last night. We'll see you soon!

Aggie turned to Twila, and said, "You called your brother?" Twila smiled and said, "I told you I was worried!" Dennis told her, "I told her not to, but she wouldn't listen. Twila hit him on the arm and said, "Traitor!" They all laughed and finished their breakfast.

It was time to take the dogs for a walk. Sharlene and Tina grabbed the dogs and headed down the road. Aggie and Twila were right behind them and the guys said they would be along after they finish their coffee. The girls were so excited to see all of the deer and asked if they could feed them. Twila told them later, we'll have to go buy some corn for them. As they were walking along, Tina pointed out there were jack rabbits by a pile of wood in the field.

As they watched, there was just a couple, then all of a sudden there must have been fifteen of them come running around the pile of wood, and jumping over each other. It looked like a herd of rabbits and they were all playing tag with each other or keep away from the deer that was standing around. It was cool to watch, Aggie had seen a few jack rabbits around, but nothing like this. Of course, they didn't bring the camera with them. Frank and Dennis came up behind them, and asked what are you guys looking at? Aggie jumped, it scared her, and she wasn't expecting them to come up behind them. Frank laughed, and Sharlene announced they were looking at jack rabbits and pointed to where they were playing. The rabbits disappeared as fast as they showed up.

They continued their walk and the kids wanted to check out the activities center. After they checked that out, they headed back to the RV. The rest of the family should be showing up soon. They went over to Twila and Dennis's trailer; they had told Frankie on the phone what section they would be in. They had just sat down at the picnic table, when they heard a couple of horns honking at them. The gangs all here!

Aggie was so happy to see everyone, she almost cried. Maria wasn't far behind. All of the kids have grown, it's only been six months, but Aggie would have sworn that they all grew three to four inches. Well all the hellos are done, now it's time to get everything set up. Frankie had cooked up some baby backs ribs and chicken for dinner tonight. They were hoping they would catch some fish to add to the meal. After everything was set up at the campground, the guys went to get some fish for dinner.

The girls just sat around and visited and looked at all the different rocks Aggie had collected on their trip so far. Enola and Treva were asking if they could have some, and Aggie said, "Of Course, this is the pile of stones you girls can pick from. There was a pretty big pile of stones from the different states they had been in, on a table Aggie had put out for them.

The guys came back with six catfish, and three bass. Frankie got busy setting up the bar-b-que and James used his grill to warm up the other meat. It sure looked like a party to Aggie. It was wonderful having all the kids visiting. While they waited for dinner to get done, they played some yard darts and cards. It's been awhile since Frank and Aggie had played cards with anyone.

After dinner they loaded up on the boats, Frankie had bought his boat too. It was a jet boat, but there won't be any skiing until tomorrow. Tonight they were just going to cruise around the lake and enjoy the evening. What a beautiful night, it was warm and the sky was as clear as could be. There must have been thousands of stars in the sky. After awhile they went back to camp and started a campfire, they wanted to roast some marshmallows and make some smores.

What a great evening, they sat around the fire and talked about the last time they were all camping together. Frankie asked his parents, "What is the deal with that old house by the gate. It looks like it could be haunted. Aggie told him, it could be, it's probably old John and Theresa. They had it built in 1881 down by the Medina River, but it had to be moved when the state decide to put the dam in, the state moved it in 1912. I'm sure John and Theresa weren't too happy about it. Frank smiled and said, "I think it is haunted!" Frank winked at Aggie. "We were checking it out the other day and it gave off a weird vibe. I got goose bumps and even your Mom could feel it.

The grandkids were all listening to Grandpa. Waiting to hear what happened next. Grandpa couldn't help it, so he continued his story. "As we were walking around the place we would hear noises calling from inside. Then we saw red hand prints on a few of the lower windows. We continued to go around the corner, when your Grandma heard something tapping on the window we had just passed. We turned back to see what it was and the red hand prints were gone. Treva asked Grandpa, "Really!" Grandpa smiled at her and continued on with his story.

We looked up at the windows where the red hands were and they were now gone and in their place were streaks of red, like someone had tried to remove them. We figured there had to be someone inside, so we put our hands up to the window to look inside and there was no one around. There was a white mist, flowing away from us and going up the stairs.

The weird feeling we had earlier became even stronger. We backed away from the house to get a better look at the upper windows of the house. It's was a huge house, it was shaped like an L. There was a balcony both in the front and the backside of the house on the second floor.

We wanted to try to go in, but the front porch didn't look all that safe, so we decided not to go on the front porch. But as we walked away, that's when I saw an old woman looking out the window on the second floor. I pointed her out to your Grandma, but she didn't see her. I thought she was kidding, but she said she really didn't see her. Grandmas interrupted Grandpa and confirmed that she didn't see any old woman.

Grandpa continued the story about the woman. She was looking out the window, with no expression on her face. I could tell she wasn't solid, the curtains flew right though her.

Now Grandpa had all of their attention. The little ones kept getting closer to their parents. Grandpa looked at them, and asked if he should stop. They all replied "No, what happened next?" Grandpa smiled and said, Ok, then! We started walking around the backside, when a piece of wood flew off the balcony and almost hit your Grandma. She moved just in time. This time Grandma saw the woman, she was dressed in early 1900's clothing. Your Grandma yelled at her, "Watch where you're throwing things." The woman had an angry look on her face and disappeared. We decided it was time to go.

We walked over to the Ranger station and told them what happened. The Ranger told us "Oh that must have been Theresa; she doesn't like people being around her house. We give tours once in awhile to people, if you want to check it out." She smiled at them as if she figured they wouldn't do it. Frank told her thanks we'll let you know.

Frankie suggested, "Maybe tomorrow we can go check it out. Frank told them, who would like to go? Everyone held their hands up accept Enola, and she said, "I don't want to see a ghost! Maria (her mom) told her, "You don't have to; we can stay home if you want!" Treva said, "Oh come on sis, I'll protect you!" James (Enola's Dad) joined in and said, "Let's see what happens tomorrow. It getting late, it's time for us to go to bed." Frank told Frankie he would check with the Ranger tomorrow about checking out the house. Maria said, "It will be interesting to check out the old house even if it's not haunted." She turned to Enola and told her, "I am sure it'll be fine!"

The grandkids; Daniel, Douglas, Sharlene and Tina were ready to go. Daniel suggested, "Maybe we should go at night, it would be more fun. Douglas had to agree with his brother; of course teenage boys would think that! Sharlene and Tina kind of agreed with them but were not too sure. The two youngest, Treva and Enola wanted to go in the daylight. Treva said, "It's an old house, maybe the floor is rotten!" She had been working with her Dad on an old house he is remodeling. James smiled your right you never know what you will find in an old house.

Aggie said we'll have to do it tomorrow. It's too late to set anything up tonight and you guys are leaving tomorrow. Well that settles it, were do it tomorrow if we get the approval from the Ranger, Frank stated. Frank followed up with, "It's "Quiet hour" in the campground, and it's time to call it a night. Everyone headed to their trailers, except Frankie and Wanda, whose trailer they were all at. They were going to stay up for a little while, and put the fire out. Treva and Enola wanted to keep Susie and Sheba for the night. Aggie agreed it would be ok, the fact that the dogs haven't left the girls side all day, had something to do with it. Aggie couldn't help thinking more room in the bed for her!

Frank and Aggie walk back to their rig. Aggie asked Frank, "Do you really think it's a good idea to take the little ones into the house?" Frank replied, "I think it'll be fine it's up to their parents.

They arrived back home and settled in for the night. It felt weird not having the dogs with them. Normally, Susi would be pulling the blankets away from Aggie, and Sheba would be barking at her. The pulling and barking would last for a few minutes, and then they would just stop. Funny how something drives you nuts, but when it not there you miss it.

The next morning Frank called the Ranger office to see if they could get a tour of the old house. The Ranger told him, they don't do tours, but he gave Frank a number to call the owner of the house. He can set up a tour with them. Frank called the number; a lady named Teri answered the phone. Frank told her what he wanted; she told him, she needed to check something first and she would be right back. After a few minutes she came back and said, "I can give you a tour at 1:00 p.m. if you like. Frank told her that would be great and hung up the phone. Frank turned to Aggie and told her, we're all set; we'll meet her at 1:00 at the house.

The next morning Frank and Aggie walked over to the kid's campsite. The guys had gone fishing first thing this morning, and were cooking them on the grill. First thing Frankie said to them was, "Well are we going to go check out the house? They were all being careful not to say "Haunted House," because of the little ones. Aggie replied yes, your Dad set it all up. We will meet Teri at the house at 1:00.

Everyone was excited about it except Enola, since she didn't want to see a ghost. Maria told her you don't have to go if don't want to. Of course, it went back and forth. First she didn't want to go and then she wanted to go.

Aggie suggested let's all go to the park and play. Off they went to the play ground. The dogs were happy to see Aggie and Frank, but Enola called them and off they went. Aggie left the kids at the play ground; she wanted to help with getting lunch ready. The older kids would keep an eye on them, besides they could see the play ground from Frankie's rig.

When lunch was ready they called the kids in, they only had to call them once. After lunch they all headed over to the old house, including Enola. She figured her Mom and Dad will protect her.

As they pulled up to the house, there was a lady waiting outside on the front porch. Aggie looked at Frank and asked, "Doesn't she look familiar to you? Frank said, "Yes!"

They all headed toward the lady, as they walked up to her, she welcomed them to the Spettel Home! I'm Teri Spettel this was my great grandparent's home. Frank couldn't help but ask, "Were you in the house on Thursday? Teri told him, "No, I haven't been out here in awhile. I only come out once and awhile to either check on the place or give a tour. Oh, we were here Thursday and we could have sworn that we saw an older you in the window. Teri smiled and said, "Yea, I hear that a lot."

Well you ready to check out the house? Teri asked. Let's do this! Frank told her. So she started to tell everyone about the history of the house. Teri explained there are a few rules; first we all stay together, no wandering off. Second don't touch anything; it's pretty dusty in there. Third if you feel someone touching you, it's ok they won't hurt you, she smiled at them.

Everyone looked at each other and Twila asked, "What? Great Grandma is protecting her house still. James turned to Frank and said, "I guess you did see someone!" This didn't help Enola; she was pulling on her Mom's arm, and said "So there is a ghost in here? Her Mom said, "I don't know, but we'll keep you safe. James reached down and picked her up, "I have you, sweetie! Enola smiled and gave her Dad a big hug.

Teri opened the door with a long creak and told everyone after you, just wait in the front room for me. They waited in the front room. Maria pointed out how much colder it was inside of the house. Twila agreed and said, "I wish I had a jacket. The front room was huge and with the stairwell on one side of the room.

Teri started to tell them the history of her family and the house. "My Great Grandfather, John Spettel, Jr. built a two-story house. It had elaborate ornamentation and it had wrap around porches when it was on the east bank of the Medina River. Grandfather was a successful cattleman and built the house for Grandma. The house was built on the south side of Mitchell's crossing on the Medina River. Drovers herding cattle from Castroville to Bandera made their way toward the Great Western Trail used the house as a rest stop. The backside of the house was used for visitors, and the help.

Teri suggested let's go this way; she continued to tell the story of the house. She was right about the dust, but even though the dust you could tell this had to be a beautiful home at one time. The reason it was moved was in 1912, they began the construction of the Medina Dam which led to the flooding of the surrounding area, including the Spettel property. Theresa chose to save the house. She couldn't stand the idea of it being at the bottom of a lake.

The house had to be cut into two pieces and was hauled to this location. It was relocated one portion at a time, and because hauling the first half by mules took nearly one month, the second half was moved with a steam engine. The Spettel family continued to use the house as their residence until 1925. The house was occupied by a subsequent family and by the mid 1940s; the former Spettel homestead was vacant.

As they walked around the house, there were doors on both sides of the fireplace; they went though the left side of the fireplace. They walked into an even larger room. Teri told them, this was the ballroom, and said this was Theresa favorite room. The fireplace in the room was made out of large sandstone, and it had access from both sides. It was huge; you could put a couple of large logs in it. Teri descried what it looked like when the house was in its prime. It had a chandelier that was made from longhorn cattle; they were form into a square, stacked on top of each other, with quartz stones hanging in the center of them. It was unusual but very pretty; Teri told them when the sun hits the stones, it was wonderful. The horns came from the cattle they had raised. John could tell you what horn came from what bull he had gotten it from.

The next room they entered into was the kitchen. It of course was huge too! It still had the old ice box and wood burning cook stove in it. They could tell the kitchen was a working kitchen. Everything looked worn, but was still in good working condition. As they were standing in the kitchen, Enola came up to Aggie. She pulled on her hand; Aggie looked down and smiled, "What's up honey?" "Grandma, can I pet the dog? Enola asked. What dog? Aggie asked. Enola pointed toward the back door and said that one! Everyone stopped talking and looked at Enola. Maria asked her, "Does it look friendly? Maria didn't what to scare her so she was trying to play it cool, while she was freaking out in her mind. Enola told her, "Yes, it's like the collie that Dad use to have. Don't you see it?' Maria had to tell her, "No, sorry!" Tina came over to Enola and told her, "I do! It's brown with black ears. Enola gave Tina a hug, Tina told her let's go pet it.

They both walked over to the area where the dog was supposed to be. But as they got closer it disappeared. Enola turned to Tina and asked, "Where did it go?" Tina said without skipping a beat, "its owner called for her." "Oh!" Enola replied, and with a sad look on her face, she walked back to her Mom. Teri didn't act surprised at all she told them, "It must have been Pepper. They had two collies, one had brown ears and one had black ears that would be Pepper. Pepper was Theresa's dog, he went everywhere with her. She passed away a little while after Theresa passed. Pepper wouldn't leave Theresa room, except on Sunday when Theresa and Pepper would walk to Church down the road, when she was alive. Well let's head upstairs, she continued with the tour, she told them that the staircase was built by John and his brothers, they used the trees from a ranch they had in the Big Bend area, and stones were from the river bed.

James couldn't help but point out the workmanship, it was amazing. Fixing up an old house has really made him appreciate the workmanship of that time. Frank had to agree with him, "It must have been beautiful when it was all shined up." When they arrived at the top of the staircase, Teri pointed toward the left, and said, "This was the master bedroom; Theresa would sit in here, and look out that window for hours, after John died. She always said she could see him walking in from the barn after a long day, he would wave at her and she always waved back."

There wasn't anything left in the bedroom accept for a large stone fireplace, it had sandstone and jasper mixed in with the river rock. It was about half the size of the one on the first floor. Aggie told Twila, I bet the fireplace kept the room nice and warm. Aggie walked over to the window, and waved for Frank to come over to the window. Aggie asked Frank, isn't this the window you saw that old woman the other day? Frank looked out the window, and turned back to Aggie, "Yes!" he pointed to the window sill and the floor around it, and the dust hadn't been disturbed. So there couldn't have been anyone standing at the window the other day. Frank started to get that weird feeling again. When Tina walked over to Aggie and told her "She is here, she's right next to Grandpa. She is smiling at him, and is trying to talk to him. It as if she knows Grandpa." Enola grabbed her Mom's hand, and said, "I see her too Mom!

Teri spoke first, "She won't hurt you, she just what's to know who's in her bedroom. Frank I think she has taken a liking to you." All Frank could come up with was, "Nice to meet you Theresa, you have a beautiful home. Thank you for letting us visits your home." Tina told Grandpa, "She says your welcome, and then disappeared! I guess she likes us!"

This whole visit Teri never seemed surprised about the ghost. Twila asked her, "Do you see a ghost?" Teri didn't answer Twila's question, it was as if she didn't what to talk about it. As they were walking through the house, nothing else happened. Until they went into John's work room, then it got a little strange.

There were a couple of work benches against the wall with a couple of hammers lying on one of the bench. Teri was talking about how John would spend hours in here, making things for the house or something for Theresa to make life better for them. As they were standing around, one of the hammers moved a little bit at first. No one was sure of what they saw, so no one said anything they just looked at each other. Then the other hammer flew up into the air and hung itself on a set of nails on the wall. This time everyone waited for Teri to say something. Which she did, "That's John, and he hates it when the workmen don't put their tools up. I guess that's where that hammer belongs" "Oh," Frank said, "Well I guess he still here." Teri had a confused look on her face; she figured they would all be running out of the house by now. Frank turned to Teri and told her; this isn't our first encounter with ghosts. With the girls seeing and hearing "ghosts," it happens they see more spirits than most families." Terri just smiled, and continued on with the tour. Frank was a little surprised she didn't say anything. Normally, people have a lot of questions.

Nothing else happened, as they finished the tour. They all were thanking Teri for taking the time to show them the house, and how great it was. As the last person came out of the house, Teri turned to Twila and the rest of the family and said, "About your question, "Do I see ghosts? Kind of … mostly because, "I am one," and with a smile she disappeared!

They all stood there in shock, then Enola laughed and said, "I'm not scared of ghosts anymore, and she was nice!" They couldn't help but laugh; James picked her up and gave her a big hug. They walked back to the car and didn't say much. Then Dennis, Twila husband spoke to Frank and Aggie, "We never have a normal day with you guys!" How did you make an appointment with a ghost anyway?" Frank replied back, "That's a good question. What can I say, we're lucky that way.

It was pretty quiet in the car on the way back to the campground. When they were back at camp, they still couldn't figure out how a ghost knew they were going to be there, and where was the real Teri that he had talked to on the phone. It was getting late and they needed to finish packing, they needed to get on the road. Hopefully, it will be light traffic for you guys! Aggie said as they were all loading up into their trucks. The way the dogs were acting they wanted to go with them, instead of staying with Aggie. The girls had put them into the truck, and Frank was trying to get them out. Finally, Frank got them, he handed Susi to Aggie and he had Sheba under control.

As they were walking back to camp Aggie kidded with Frank, it looks like you have an admirer. Theresa "the ghost" threw that piece of wood at me, because she wanted you. Frank laughed and told Aggie, "I think you don't have anything to worry about! Hopefully, she can't follow us!" They walked back to their place and settled in for the night.

Aggie checked her voice mail and she had one message. She didn't recognize the number, as she listened to the voice mail, she couldn't believe what she was hearing. She told Frank, you're not going to believe this, listen to this! Frank took the phone, and this was what he heard, "Hi, this is Teri, my car broke down, so I won't be making it to the house today. Please give me a call and we can set up something later, if you like." Frank told Aggie, "Well that explains how the ghost was waiting for us, instead of Teri."

The next morning Frank and Aggie couldn't stand it, they went over to the ranger office, and told the ranger what happen. All she said was, "I'll be damned, not everyone gets a tour by Alice, she is the daughter of John and Theresa, she lived in it until she died. She always said her parents were living with her even after they died. That's why she never moved into the master bedroom. I guess they all live there together. I've seen her couple of times, but she never showed up as a human before." Aggie just smiled and said, I guess we're just lucky that way.

Well thanks for the information. As they walked back to the camp, they looked over at the old house and on the porch stood John, Theresa and Alice (aka Teri) waving at them. Aggie waved back. Frank told Aggie just keeps walking; we don't need them following us home, Aggie laughed and kept walking.

The next couple of weeks were nice and quiet; they did a lot of walking about the campground, they decided to stay away from the old house.

There are a lot of little towns in the area; they wanted to visit a few of them. They enjoyed wandering around the little towns and learning their history. They would pack a picnic lunch and just drive. The girls (dogs) really enjoyed going for rides. Susi would look out the window the whole time, it was kind of weird but she did enjoy it! Sheba on the other hand would lie on her blanket and wait for the car to stop; so she could go for a walk. She didn't care where, as long as it was some place different.

They had forgotten how bad the storms could be in Texas in the spring time, with the driving rains and the winds. They watched the lake water go up and down for the last three weeks, there was a little island so they could gage the water level against.

They had one more day to kill, so they decided to go to Comfort, TX. They had heard it was a small town with a lot of history. As they drove around town they spotted a twenty-foot obelisk, in a park area. They pulled over to see what it was all about. It was a dedication to the German Patriots that died in combat, fighting for the union in the Civil War. According to the sign, "The monument was erected in1866, to honor the memory of 68 men, which were mostly Germans though they lived in a confederate state. They were loyal to the union during the civil war."

"They desperately tried to reach U.S. Federal troops by way of Mexico. About 40 of the men were killed by vengeful confederates bent on annihilating them, in the battle of the Nueces in 1862. The bodies of the slain and those who drowned swimming the Rio Grande were left unburied."

"A group of Germans from the town gathered the bones of their friends and buried them at the site in 1865. The flag that flew over the monument was a United State flag with thirty six stars. It did look a little strange; it was the banner at the time of the monument dedication in 1866."

It was a very solemn place, as they walked around looking at the stone; each side of the obelisk had a list of names that had died at the attack. They could tell the town was very proud of their ancestors.

Frank was getting hungry; they headed into downtown to find someplace to eat. They found a small pizza place on a corner in downtown. It wasn't too bad, Aggie told Frank she was surprise how many Germans were in Texas. Frank replied, "Yea, I guess their everywhere!" After lunch they headed back to camp, and started to break down camp.

It was time to move on, next stop Colorado River Campground; it was about six miles from Columbus. Frank had been talking to one of the Rangers about the next stop, and she told him, he should call ahead to make sure the road was open. They have been having a lot of flooding in that area. Aggie called the new site the day before, and the Ranger told her the roads were fine. The plan was on, next stop Colorado River campground.

As usual they packed everything up the day before, all they had to do is break down the electric, water and sewage, after breakfast. They learned from the last move, to eat before heading out. Just in case it took longer to arrive at their new location than they had planned.

The morning of the move, Aggie looked out the side window and there stood three white tail bucks, they all had a four point rack on them. They were beautiful! It's funny how the bucks all hang together after mating season. Otherwise, they would be fighting for the attention of the females.

After breakfast Frank went out to do his thing and Aggie finished getting the inside ready for traveling. Twenty minutes later they were ready to go. The weather forecast said it wasn't going to rain today, but another big storm was coming their way. It was coming from the west and they were heading up north away from the storm. They were glad they would be settled in before the next big storm hit.

It took them three hours to get to Columbus, TX. The campground was only six miles away from Columbus. They took the loop around San Antonio, and then headed to Columbus, TX. Aggie spotted the turn to late for Frank to make the turn, so he had to go up to the next turn off and come back. Then three miles down a back road, they saw the sign, you couldn't miss it. After diving around the campground for awhile they finally found a suitable place to set up camp.

The weather woman reported that there was a large storm coming from the west, with high winds and heavy rain. They decided not to put up the screen room and keep everything stored under the RV until after the storm. There was a nice hiking trail; so they took the girls out for a walk. About half way through the walk, Sheba just sat down, and refused to move. Aggie picked her up and they continued the walk. Three miles later they were back at camp.

The next morning the sky started to change, from a clear sky to a sky with large black clouds and the wind was starting to pick up. By noon the front part of the storm hit, lighting and thunder and then the rain. It was a driving rain with big rain drops, they looked a lot like hail stones. It stormed into the night, and the rain didn't stop.

The next day, it was the same. The Colorado River was filling up and by three PM. It wouldn't be the first time the river had flooded: they didn't what to take any chances. Frank and Aggie was on the upper part of camp sites. They couldn't see the river from where they were located. There were two rigs left that needed to be moved, the people that owned them wasn't around. As the water continued to rise the water started going under the two rigs.

Frank and Aggie watched from their rig as the events unfolded; there wasn't anything they could do to help. The rain had let up a little; at least they could see what was going on. Originally there was six feet of land behind each of the rigs, but the land started to go down into the river, now there was only three. The bank continued to slide into the Colorado River, inch by inch. Two large trucks arrived to remove the last two rigs, and they backed up to the fifth wheels. The first one started to pull out the rig, but it got stuck in the mud. The driver gunned the truck and the rig jumped forward, the rig was free, and he pulled it up the hill.

During that short amount of time, the three feet turned into one foot and the back of the second rig was hanging over the edge. There was three inches of water under the fifth wheel by now. The guy that was pulling this rig was ready to go, everyone backed away from the rig and the truck. He put the truck into low, and pulled as hard as he truck could. His tires were spinning in the water and then the tires took hold. The truck and rig pulled forward with a lunge. It looked like the truck jumped two feet in the air, and then the rig followed the truck up the hill. Everyone was cheering and clapping as he pulled away.

The rain started to pour down heavier than it had done earlier. Everyone started to go back to their rigs. Then all of a sudden the rest of the bank gave way. There were three people standing by the edge still, one person jumped back just in time and the other two started going down with the mud. But the mud slide stopped for a second and the two climbed up the hill with the help of a rope someone had thrown to them. The campground lost three spaces that night, they were just happy everyone got out of there safe.

What a day, rain, heavy rain and 40 to 45 mph winds. Frank and Aggie ended up watching movies that night, because the satellite couldn't get any signal thought the heavy cloud cover. Because of the wind Penelope rocked back and forth most of the night; the rain did finally stop around 1:00 a.m.

The next morning the sun was pushing its way out of the clouds, the wind was just a breeze. The girls were ready to go outside; Frank let them out, while Aggie got their coffee. They walked down to where all the action had been going on the night before. The slide had taken out the whole area the four RV's had been parked at. But the river still ran high; the water had reached in land about 200 feet. They were smart to move everyone from the lower area. There was no way anyone would have saved their rigs otherwise.

Every day the water receded, by the end of the week the lower part was all mud where the water had flooded. There were a few catfish and blue gills that got stuck on land. As they walked along the edge they could see green slime everywhere. It looked like algae that had washed to the shore from the river. It was starting to stink, the mud and whatever else that came from the river was drying out.

After hanging around the campground for the last week because of the weather, they were starting to get cabin fever. It was a beautiful day; there was no way they were just going to hang out around the campground. So they decided to go visit Columbus, according to the Columbus web site it was a very historical area.

They drove over to the old downtown which was only six miles away. They had been to the newer part of Columbus earlier that week, but now they wanted to check out old town.

In the center of downtown was the "Colorado County Courthouse, it was constructed in 1890-1891 in the form of a Greek cross. The courthouse reflects the style of the period with its combination of French Second Empire, Renaissance Revival and Italianate influences. The roof and tower of the courthouse were destroyed in a storm in 1901 and replaced with the classical detailing and a center dome,"

At first Frank and Aggie just walked around the courthouse, and around the court yard. The streets were lined with old buildings, from the mid 1800's that were still being used. The buildings were amazing and well maintained; there was history on every side. Aggie told Frank, let's go check out the courthouse, they were not sure if it was open or not, but what the heck.

It turned out it was open and it was amazing inside. There were doors going down each side of the hallway, they were at least 10 feet tall. To the right there was a massive staircase, it was made out of dark oak wood. There was no one to be seen, but it was still a working courthouse. They wandered down to the bottom floor, where the restrooms were. The hallway there was all white, with white benches that looked like steps along the length of the hallway, except where there were doorways. The lighting made the area glow, it was a little eerie, but striking at the same time. Aggie felt like she should be quiet and not touch anything.

They were getting ready to leave the courthouse, when they ran into a lady that worked in the courthouse; she asked if she could help them. Aggie told her they were just visiting. She asked if they had been up to see the dome or in the main courtroom. They told her no, she told them you really should check it out. She pointed up the stairs and explained where to go. They thanked her and headed up to the courtroom and where the dome was suppose to be, which was on the third floor.

As they came around the corner of the staircase, there were to huge dark oak doors entrance way. They walked into the courtroom, they couldn't believe their eyes. The courtroom looked like it came out of a Perry Mason show. As they looked around and then looked up they saw the dome.

The dome was made out of beautiful stained glass. It was done in mostly different colors of green and gold trim. With the sun coming in, the dome glowed and gave off different colors of lights. It also had a chandelier that hung from the center of the dome, which looked like a green umbrella hanging upside down. It was incredible, like everything else in the courthouse. They were glad they came inside to see the courthouse.

They had gotten a historical map from the Chamber of Commerce, so they explored more of the town. They drove around the town; there were many things to see. They even found the 2nd largest oak tree in Texas, according to the sign, the circumference of the trunk is 329 inches and it is 70 feet tall. It is estimated to be 500 years old, or older, it's kind of hard to tell without cutting it down. It is a remarkable tree; they even had iron posts to hold up some of the huge sagging branches.

Next they headed to the town of La Grange; it was about twenty miles north. It didn't take long to get there, when you go 70 mph. They had read that "The German immigration came after the Mexican revolutions of 1848. The town was a major site of German settlement; they said the rolling hills and forests were reminiscent of their homelands. The German and Czech influences on the town are still visible in many local customs, the architecture.

They found a parking space in front of the town courthouse. From the parking lot the courthouse looked like a small castle, it had huge trees all around it. They walked inside; there was a hallway that went into a courtyard, which was in the middle of the courthouse. In the courtyard, there were white bricks that went all the way up to a dome and around the courtyard, and as they looked up they saw a sky light. The sky light was huge but it was just clear glass, nothing like the one in Columbus.

The walls had arched windows, with no glass in them, they faced the courtyard and there were hallways going around the courtyard. There were three floors; each wall had three arched windows, with a screen in the lower part of the window. Aggies figure it was to stop people from jumping or falling. In the center of the courtyard was a large three bowl fountain, which looked like something you would see in Germany. This courthouse wasn't as beautiful as the courthouse in Columbus, but it was unique in its own right.

Frank and Aggie were walking out of the courthouse, when Aggie spotted an old bakery. She told Frank lets go check it out, as they were walking across the street, they heard a loud noise. They turned to see this huge tractor coming down the road. They could only see the top part of it, but as it got closer, they saw that the tires were as tall as their Jeep. Behind the larger tractor, there was a line of smaller tractors following it. Frank and Aggie just looked at each other, when Aggie said; I guess their having a parade! Frank replied, "I guess, but there's no one around to watch it.

Weird! Aggie said as they walked into the Bakery. She asked the lady at the counter, what's with the tractors going through town? She told Aggie, "Oh they are moving their business to a bigger site on the other side of town. They are just driving their equipment to the new site.

They figured instead of paying to load the equipment on trailers and moving them, it would be cheaper to drive them. So they hired the 4H members to help move most of their equipment. The bigger equipment they had to drive around the town, on the back road. It's been interesting to watch!"

Frank was looking at all the bakery goods while she was talking. There wasn't a lot left; of course it was mid afternoon. Frank pointed out a few things he wanted and Aggie took the last of the cinnamon rolls for breakfast tomorrow.

Aggie asked the lady at the counter, how long has she been working at the bakery and how long has it been here. The lady told Aggie, that her family had owned this business for 100 years. Her great grandparent had started it and lived upstairs. Now she's the last of her family, so it won't be around much longer.

They thanked her and headed out the door. Aggie told Frank it's always sad to see an old business go to the way side because their kids don't what to deal with it. Frank agreed with her.

It was a short drive home, they saw all kinds of BBQ places to eat at, but they weren't hungry. They kind of wished that they were! There were a few places that looked interesting. One thing about Texas they do love their BBQ.

When they arrived home both Sheba and Susi were at the window barking like crazy. They always sit on the dashboard, and look out the wind shield when they are gone. This meant they would be going for a walk, before doing anything else. As Frank opened the door, Susi came flying out and heading for a tree. Sheba just barked and waited for Aggie to pick her up and put her on the ground. Aggie had to laugh to herself, she knows Sheba can get down the steps, but she won't if someone is standing there.

They did the short walk with Sheba and put her back into the RV and then started going for a longer walk with Susi. It ended up being a lot longer walk then they had planned. After about two miles, they ended up back at the Activate Center at the campground. Even Susi was getting tired, so they got some water for them and Susi. They relaxed for a little bit on a bench outside the center before going home. They still had another half mile to go to the RV, and there wasn't any way they were going to carry Susi.

After Susi had her drink and was rested, she was ready to go again. Aggie wishes she could say the same thing. As usual, Sheba started barking at Susi when they arrived home, because Susi got to go with them. Sheba really doesn't like going for long walks, she will stop and refuse to move when she is done walking. Then they would have to carry her home. But she does enjoy barking at Susi. Sheba waited to be picked up by Aggie, and then life was good again.

The weather was finally nice for a whole week; no wind or rain. The rest of their stay looked like it was going to be nice and quiet. In the morning the deer would come though the fields and the birds would be singing. There were so many types of birds; Aggie wished she had a bird book sometimes so she could identify them.

Spring Break was next week; they assumed it would be packed with families and lots of kids. But even spring break wasn't that bad. Most of the families set up in the lower part by the playground. Frank and Aggie love their kids and grandkids, but they did enjoy the quiet. Screaming and yelling kids really isn't their thing anymore. Susi doesn't like it to much either; she will start barking every time she hears a kid scream or yell. Nice thing it's only for a week.

Later on after the kids were gone, Frank and Aggie were going on one of their walks along the river. As they were looking over to the island which was on the other side of the river, they spotted something. There were six shining looking disks laying on the edge of the island not far from the water's edge.

Aggie pointed them out to Frank, who has eagle eyes. He told her they were turtles. He couldn't tell what type they were, but they were at least six inches across.

Aggie suggested they go back to the rig and get their binoculars. Frank agreed with her. They walked back to the rig and got the binoculars and left Susi in the RV. Then they headed back to where they had spotted the turtles earlier.

The turtles were still lying out in the sun. Aggie raised her binocular and sure enough they were turtles. They were as big as a Frisbee, but now there were eight of them. As they looked out at the island, Frank pointed out that there were at least fifteen little ones lying out there with the big ones.

A couple that was walking by, stopped and asked them what they were looking at? Aggie with excitement in her voice said, "Turtles, lots of turtles!" Then she pointed toward the island. Aggie offered her binocular to the lady, whose name was Peggy, so she could see the turtles better. Frank offered his to the guy, his name was Jose. They had met the couple earlier in the week when they would be out walking their dog.

Peggy got so excited, she told Aggie, "They are so big and the little ones are all over the place. Just as she said it, a Heron flew over the top of the island, and within a manner of seconds all of the turtle were gone! Frank said, "I guess they know what that shadow means!"

Aggie couldn't help herself she said, "Damn bird!" Peggy agreed with her, Peggy raised her fist and shook it at the bird. They all laughed! Peggy and Jose thanked them for sharing, and continued on their walk.

Frank and Aggie watched for a little longer waiting to see if the turtles would come back, but they got bored and decided to go home and have dinner. They had missed lunch, so it was an early dinner for them tonight.

Tomorrow was pack up day, and then on Thursday, they would be heading to Lake Conroe.

CHAPTER 15

———◆◆◆◆◆◆◆———

Camping in Central Texas

I t didn't take long to get to Lake Conroe; it wasn't hard to find the campground this time. The roads weren't too bad, but the spaces were not the best. Frank and Aggie found a nice place by a pond; it was in between to annual people.

An annual person is someone that leases a spot for one year. They can either live there full time or leave their rig and just come and visit once-in-awhile. Each campground that they have been too has had more and more of this type of sites. Frank and Aggie always tried to park by one of these spot, more than likely they won't have weekend neighbors. Which normally has kids or to enjoy the weekend with parties. Funny Aggie remembers those days, and how times have changed.

Each of the campgrounds that they had stayed at in Texas has been huge. Lake Conroe wasn't any different; it had over 477 parking spaces. They had updated their pool and restroom areas. It was the nicest they had been to as far as the pool and restroom. But the roads and parking space wasn't that great. All the rain had made little water ways going down the roads. Like the other campgrounds in Texas, this one was on a lake too. It was Lake Conroe, and it was a huge lake. It also had two ponds; which they parked their rig by one of them. The closest town was Willis; it was a nice little town. But there wasn't much to see there.

The first week was quiet and not very many people around. But when the weekend arrived it filled up pretty quick. They discovered their mistake of parking near the cabins and the fishing pond, later on that evening.

Two of the cabins must have been rented by the same group. They were BBQ between the two cabins and running back and forth to each other's place. As the day turned into night, the group got louder and louder. From what Aggie heard it was George's 21st birthday. Aggie had to wonder how long the party was going to go on. Quite time is 11:00 p.m., and sure enough at 11, everything went silent! She looked over at the cabin and they were still all there, it was kind of weird. Just like magic, the yelling and loud music stopped. Frank had been sleeping through the whole thing. Aggie headed to bed, while it was still quiet!

The rest of their time at Lake Conroe was pretty low key, the rain and wind had followed them. They took walks in between the rain storms; there wasn't much to do otherwise. The lake water was up by two feet and the docks were almost underwater. They did have a crawfish feast at the campground, which they went to. There was enough crawfish to sink a boat or two.

Afterwards they walked down to the docks, and the water had come up another foot. They saw splashing across the water; it looked like something getting attacked in the water. It reminded them of piranha fish feeding; the splashing would go up and down the lake bank. Then the splashing happens in the dock area. All they saw were large red tail fins coming out of the water.

Aggie asked a couple that was fishing nearby, what was doing all of the splashing. They told them it was carp, their eating the worms and bugs off the flooded banks and docks. As if to show them that they were there, the bank of the island came alive. Splashing, they could see three or four red tails in the air. It was a little freaky! Aggie saw a few ducks head into the water, she was waiting for the carp to attack, but the carp were too busy eating bugs off the banks, she guessed.

Each day was getting hotter and more humid, and the girls were getting tired of it. Sheba was having more trouble than Susie, she has heart issues. It was harder for her to breathe. They knew that when they adopted her, but she was a sweetie, they didn't care.

They had been watching the news about all the flooding in the area around Houston. They had been talking to their kids, and everything was ok in their area so far. Frank Jr. had told them the water has gotten close to the backyard a couple of times. But they had sand bags stacked five high to protect the lower part of their property. He told them they didn't need to come home; they will call if anything happens. Aggie suggested they could come home for the weekend and visit, if they like. Frankie said, "That would be great!" He'll let the girls know, and we'll have a BBQ.

After talking to Frankie, it made Aggie homesick. Frank and Aggie decided to go home for the day. It really wasn't a hard choice; the weekend at the RV camp ground was crazy, but they did enjoy hanging out with the family.

It was a short drive to Houston; it was nice they could do a day trip, instead of spending the night away from Penelope. They have gotten pretty attached to her. It was nice waking up in the same bed every morning, but yet they could look out in the morning and have a new view. It's so much better than a hotel.

They left early to beat the traffic, it was a beautiful day. As they pulled into Frankie's place, all the grandkids came running out. Aggie and Frank were greeted with big hugs and being told how much they had missed them. Aggie couldn't believe it has only been a month since they had seen them. She could have sworn they all grew another foot.

Frank was wondering where their kids were. As they both walked into Frankie's house. All the grandkids were all around them, talking and laughing at the same time. As they walked into the living room there sat their children. They all waved and said Hi! Aggie was getting a little upset, she had to wonder, and didn't they miss them. What the heck she thought to herself!

Then they all jumped up and ran over to them, laughing. Wanda couldn't help it and told them, "It was Frankie's idea, to just sit there and act like they didn't miss them. You should have seen your faces!" Maria said, as she still was laughing, while she was hugging her mom.

After the hugging and hellos were done, Aggie grabbed Frankie's ear and pinched it. She called him a "Little Shit!" They all started laughing again, as Frankie tried to pull away from his Mom.

The rest of the afternoon was great. They went over to Maria and James house to see all the remodeling they have done. Frank was telling James and Maria what a great job they were doing on the remodeling when a shelf on the wall fell down. James told them, "I was planning on taking it down anyway." Maria turned to James and said, "Well one less thing to do, as she picked up the shelf and put it on the table. It was time to head back to Frankie and Wanda's place for dinner.

As usual it was a great BBQ; they had ribs and fish, with all the fixin'. After dinner it was time to head back to Lake Conroe, it was great to see all the kids.

There had been flooding in the area they were planning on driving home on, so they were going to have to change their travels and take the long way home. It didn't take long for the dogs to settle down in the car, the grandkids kept them pretty busy the whole day.

It took an extra hour to get home, but it was great to see all of the family. They normally break down the day before, but it was getting late so they decided to pack and travel all the same day. They were only going to go 157 miles in one day. Their next stop was Lake Tawakoni. Lake Conroe was nice but a little too busy for them. They were hoping Lake Tawakoni would be a little slower pace.

There was going to be a big storm coming later in the afternoon, so they wanted to leave early enough to miss it. They got everything packed a couple days earlier, because of the rainstorms that came in and out during the week. So there were just a few things to be packed up, the day of the move.

They pulled out of their space and headed out of the campground. The sky had dark clouds in the distance; they looked like the clouds they have been seeing all week. It was coming from the northwest. Their next campground was north. They were hoping to be at the campsite before the storm hit. According to the weather man the storm would be around for three days and will be heavy rains and thunderstorms.

As they were driving the wind started to pick up and the storm clouds were moving straight at them. Aggie radioed Frank and told him, "I don't think we're going to beat the storm!" Frank radioed back, "Your right the rain is coming down in front of me!" Aggie was behind him so she couldn't see what he was talking about. But five minutes later she found out. It was like she had driven into a waterfall. She was glad that Frank was in front of her. All she could see was the back of Penelope. She may not see the road but she could just follow Frank. It was crazy how trucks and cars were driving pass them. She had to wonder how they could see anything.

It continued to pour for the next twenty miles. The rain stopped as fast as it started. It was amazing as she pulled out of the waterfall there was the sun, and it was dry.

She radioed Frank, "Is that it?" He replied back, "Yea, it's clear as far as I can see. Go ahead and take the lead if you what." As Aggie started to pass Frank she looked in her rearview mirror, and she could see the rain and dark clouds behind her. There is nothing like Texas rainstorms, everything is bigger in Texas!

It took another hour before they arrived at their new campground. They pulled up to the Rangers building to check in. While they were checking in the Ranger told them to keep an eye out for snakes. Because of all the flooding they have been coming into the campground. They had to kill five of them earlier during the week.

After driving around for awhile, they found a place to park. A lot of the park was flood. Aggie parked the Jeep, and walked around the space to check for snakes. She then got on the walkie talkie and told Frank, "I don't see any snakes, come on back, and turn to the right a little bit, looking good!" Frank started backing up the rig; she got a weird feeling that someone or something was watching her. She had checked the ground but hasn't looked up in the trees. As she started to look up, sure enough a snake was hanging off a branch.

Frank was still backing up, when he heard Aggie scream. He stopped the rig and tired to see Aggie in the outside mirror but couldn't. He called her on the walkie talkie "Aggie are you alright?" Aggie heard Frank voice. At this point she replied to him, "Frank we have a problem, you need to come out here, make sure the dogs stay in the RV. Come around on the driver side!" Aggies's voice sound weird, Frank radio back "What's going on?" Aggie replied back, "We have a very large snake!" What! On my way, Frank replied into the radio. Frank did as Aggie had told him, and he came around the corner, but he still hasn't seen Aggie. As he got closer to the end of the RV, he saw Aggie. She had a large stick in one hand and was pointing at the back of the RV. He turned the corner and looked up where Aggie had been pointing.

He couldn't believe what he was seeing. A five foot Copperhead snake, it was crawling onto the top of the RV. Part of it was just hanging there on the branch and laying it's head on the RV. Frank and Aggie just looked at each other, then back at the snake. It started to move down the ladder that was part of the RV.

Frank looked back at Aggie and all he could say was, "What the hell?" She replied back, "I guess he needs a ride, she smiled at him. They just stood there for a little bit, as it slowly started to climb down the ladder.

Aggie turned to Frank and told him, "It looks like it might take a little while. What about him, Aggie pointed to the snake crawling on their RV. Frank told her, "He should be down in a couple of minutes. I don't think we what to upset it, or hurt him.

Aggie smiled at him and handed him her stick and said, "Here you go, keep an eye on the snake. I'll take the Jeep and find us a new space, I'll be right back." Frank smiled, "Ok!" Aggie headed to the Jeep.

Frank was watching the snake. It had crawled out of the tree and was halfway down the RV ladder. He thought to himself, "Only in Texas!" Then he told the snake, "Well how has your day been going?" As if the snake heard him, it stopped and raised its head up and looked at him. Then it continued on down the ladder. It hung at the end of the ladder, and then it just dropped to the ground. After a few second it started to crawl away into the woods.

Frank stood very still, he didn't what to kill the snake, and he was pretty sure the snake would agree with him. As it crawled into the bushes, Frank couldn't help think how fat and health it looked.

Once it was gone, Frank headed back into the front of the RV. Where Aggie had just pulled up and she yelled to him, that she found them a new place to park on the other side of the park. She smiled and said, "Sorry no snakes this time! I looked high and low this and found nothing!" Frank smiled and told her lead the way, he got into the RV and followed her to their new location.

They got to the other location they both walked around the area to make sure there were no snakes before they let the dogs out. A Copperhead that size could have killed them. Once they were sure there were no snakes, they let the girls come out. As soon as they were let out the girls ran around and checked out their new place.

It didn't take long for them to set up camp; the girls did their normal thing at a new location. They ran around and checked out the area and everything looked ok to them. It's a great spot Frank told Aggie. It has a great view. There was a large field in front of them and woods around them. They could see the Ranger station from their site, which was the entrance way into the park. It was always interesting to watch the people come and go.

The weekends were the crazies; Aggie called the people that came on the weekend short timer. They would hurry around trying to find a spot, set up, start a fire and break out the beer. The kids would ride their bikes up and down the road, and yell and scream.

On the week days the park would empty out. Then the full timer and annual would have the place to themselves again. Frank and Aggie could only imagine what it was like in the summer time at any of the campground they have been to so far. They only have experienced the campgrounds in the winter so far on this adventure. Other then Spring break and three day weekends, they got a taste of what it would be like.

After getting everything set up, Frank was feeling really tired. He decided to take a nap, before they went for their walk. It was unusual for him to take a nap turning the day. He had been complaining about he wasn't feeling to good, for the last few weeks. Aggie figurer he was getting the flu or something.

After Franks nap, he felt better and was ready to go for their walk. But he still didn't look all that great. But they headed out to explore their new home anyway. With the campground map in hand they headed to the activities center, which was on the other side of the campground. Sheba was still tired from the earlier walk with Aggie, so they only took Susi. Susi was always ready for a walk.

Some of the camp sites were still under water, all you could see is the power connection poles. Hopefully, they were all turned off before they were flood, Aggie had told Frank earlier.

One of the annual sites had their satellite dish about twenty feet away from their rig and it was in about two feet of water now. It looked pretty funny standing out in the mid of the water. Aggie made a crack to Frank, "Maybe the fish are using it!" Frank smiled and told her, "You never know!"

It was understandable why the snakes were coming into the campground. There wasn't anywhere else to go! Frank and Aggie kept Susi close to them and one eye looking out for any snakes. What they did see a lot of were turtles and frogs. There were all sizes; big one, little one, and all types around the campground.

Aggie found one turtle that had been ran over by the lawn motor. Half of it was clean and the other half had grass on it. It looked like it was trying to get to the pond, which was about twenty feet away. She picked it up and it looked fine. So she carried it to the pond and put it at the edge of the water. It didn't move, so she put it half in the water and half on land. That's all it took, it stuck its head out, and it was gone. Not even a thank you or good bye.

They stood looking around the pond, when they spotted frogs line up around the pond. It was weird every two feet there was a frog sitting all around one side of the pond. As they continue to watch they could see turtle heads popping up. They looked at each other, when Frank said, "Maybe they're going to fight, and I think the frog is going to lose!"

They watched for a little longer, but nothing happen, they continued on their walk. There was another pond and the lake not too far from where they were at.

At the next pond, there wasn't much action, they think they spotted a couple of water moccasins, but it was hard to tell. Next stop the Activities center; they took turns going in, because dogs were not permitted in. It was a huge center, and looked liked they had a lot of activities in the summer for the kids.

Frank was getting tired so they headed back home. As they were walking Frank told Aggie, "After this I think we should go home for awhile, don't you?" Aggie smiled and said, "You need to stop reading my mind!"

They both admitted they were missing the family, and how great it was to enjoy the grandkids. Aggie pointed out how big they are getting, and the house looked like it needed some work. It would be nice to get out on the ocean for a few days too. As they walked home, they came up with more and more reason to go home, and less reason continue on the travels. Aggie told Frank, just for a few months, and then we'll have to go see the rest of the country. Frank agreed, "Yea, we still have too much to see! They arrived at their RV, and sat outside. They started a fire and talked about all the great things they have seen in the last year.

Locations they visited

Oregon

Oregon Coast:

Florence, Sea Lion Caves, Pacific City, Cape Kiwanda Park, Munson Falls, Tillamook Air Museum and Pioneer Museum, Kilchis Point, Cape Look Out State Park, Cape Meares Light house, Octopus tree, Fort Yamhill, Brownville,

Central Oregon:

Bend, Lava River cave, Mount Bachelor, High Desert Museum

Crater Lake National Park, Phantom Ship Overlook, Pinnacles Overlook, Vidae Falls, Newberry National Volcanic Monument, Paulina Falls, Burns

Idaho: Nampa, Twin Falls

Nevada: Lowell Lake, Ely, Alamo, Nolan County

Utah: Dixie Center Wildlife Museum

Arizona: Kingman, McMullen Valley, Cottonwood list in Chapter 10, Benson area has a lot to see too: Ft. Huachuca, Fairbank Historic Town, Amerind Museum & Art Gallery, Kartchner Caverns, and Tombstone.

New Mexico: Deming Luna Mimbers Museum, and City of the Rocks State Park.

Texas: Trans Mountain viewport, Camp Stockton, Fort Stockton, Medina River Thousands Trails campground, Spettel Haunted House, Comfort, Columbus River, LaGrange, Lake Conroe, and Point.

Printed in the United States
By Bookmasters